Between the Dragon and His Wrath

K-Nurse, Book Four

By Mark Leo Tapper

Sousa House Press
Barre, Vermont 05641

Copyright © 2022 by Mark Leo Tapper and Sousa House Press.

All rights reserved. No portion of this book may be reproduced in any form without the express written permission of the author. Printed in the United States of America.

This book is a work of fiction. All characters, names, places, and events are a product of the author's imagination or are used fictitiously. Any resemblance to persons living or dead, companies or events is entirely coincidental.

ISBN: 978-0-9989066-8-3

Cover design by Marianne Nowicki

For John Drain and Mark Grieco,

brothers from another mother

"Come not between the dragon and his wrath."

King Lear, Act 1, Scene 1

One

Messina, Italy, 1347

I covered my hand with my robe before smoothing lank hair away from the old man's forehead. He was drenched in sweat and murmuring nonsense, a sure sign that death was not far away. When he twitched and kicked at the blanket, the black boils on his legs showed, looking like the ball of a spider's eggs. I pulled the blanket back over them, telling myself it would keep the pestilence from spreading, but in truth, it was because the sight of those boils made my blood run cold.

Andrew was nearby, giving last rites to people lying on the ground, some, no doubt already dead. An old woman leaning against the wall coughed, spraying a fountain of blood, before collapsing. Throughout the church people murmured prayers. *"Pater noster qui es in caelis . . ."* Every few hours horse-drawn carts arrived, and men with cloths wrapped around their faces would take the bodies away.

Day and night turned over and over, like the flow of water over a stone in the river. The Church of the Santissima Annunziata dei Catalani held us against its cool stone breast, the dome and tiled stars so much like our old church in Jerusalem. We laid the afflicted on the ground in the apse, and while the stone sheltered us from the Sicilian heat, it did nothing to lessen the stench of death or the panic and exhaustion that infused every waking moment.

Sitting under the great crucifix behind the altar, Andrew and I picked at a loaf of stale bread and sipped altar wine while Philip and Bartholomew administered to our flock.

"The Lord is punishing us for our wickedness. That much is certain," I said before dipping the bread into my cup.

"The Lord," Andrew huffed. "The Lord our God, slaughterer of the innocents."

"He has before. He permitted Herod to kill hundreds of babies to protect the Christ. We do not question the choices God makes, Father."

"Oh yes," Andrew said, "our loving and merciful God didn't lift a finger while sucking babes were put to the sword. What rubbish."

"Father Andrew," I whispered, "be careful. There are those who would say that's heresy."

"*Si*," Andrew replied. "Look around you, Paul. Do you see God's hand here?"

"I see God's hand in everything."

"Then you are a fool, Brother Paul. Sister Augustine died last night," he said, his face a mask of grief.

"She was in fine health yesterday morning." I made the sign of the cross. "She'll be back with us soon enough."

"I was in fine health yesterday morning," Andrew said, lifting the woolen sleeve of his robe. A line of small, black pustules was forming along his shoulder, one of them oozing pus.

The weight of the endless days spent among the boils and the terror was a yoke I could not bear without faith and without Andrew. Andrew said nothing as he pulled his sleeve back down.

People shuffled into the church from doors beside and behind the altar. They looked for open places on the floor to lie down and die.

The creaking wheel of another cart announced its arrival beyond the wooden doors. When they opened, the bright sunlight blinded us.

Two

I stayed focused on what my hands were doing, despite the fog on my faceshield. Find the vein. Bounce it under my left index finger. With my right index finger, push the needle just under my left finger. See a flash of blood in the needle chamber. Tap the button to retract the needle, leaving the little plastic tube, the cannula, in the vein. Click the cannula housing into a butterfly device that sticks to the skin, and voila, a new peripheral intravenous access was born.

Now we could pump all manner of drugs or fluids or blood products directly into the patient's vascular system.

For what it was worth.

More than half of the people we worked on in trauma bay six were dead before we injected the medicine that might keep them alive.

Thomas put a number three Macintosh blade down the patient's throat, hooking it into the trachea to intubate the patient. For civilians, he used a long, dull, hooked piece of metal to separate the windpipe from the esophagus so that he could put a tube down the windpipe. Then, a machine could breathe for this poor soul, who now had an IV in each arm, a tube down his throat, and a catheter in his penis.

Like the others who had rumbled through trauma bay six, his eyes were swollen shut, his neck puffed up like an angry chicken. His fingers and toes had become grotesque sausages with blue-purple nails. He was a flesh balloon at the point of popping. James set the respirator, and Andrew programed the IV pump, before two orderlies in hazmat whites pushed the patient away and brought us a new one, this time a little girl who was already dead.

James turned away, and his shoulders trembled. I signaled for the orderly to take the girl to the morgue and bring us another patient. The new one arrested before Thomas could intubate her. We got the next three all tubed up before hitting a bad patch of nine corpses in a row.

The floor of the trauma bay was so littered with packaging and wrappings from all of the supplies we used, that the carts crunched on the debris coming and going. At some point housekeeping would sweep some of this away, but there were so few of them left.

The skin where my ears met my head was raw and open from hours of rubber straps on the mask I wore under the faceshield. I couldn't remember the last time I had used the bathroom. My lips cracked behind the mask, and my own breath was making me nauseous.

We are the Knight Nurses of the Order of St. John. We know death and suffering. Our lives have been nine hundred years of enduring an endless parade of it. James had not been in the nursing trenches in a couple of lifetimes, having found his way to more administrative, and, ultimately, computer-oriented duties. He was a good clinical nurse though, and the current state of the world demanded all hands on deck. James was out of practice, and he was taking it hard.

My paper booties wore through early on, and I knew they would make me dispose of the sneakers underneath at the end of my shift, the third pair this week.

Whenever I flagged, I looked to Thomas for inspiration. He was a machine. He had the hardest job, the delicate task of placing a breathing tube. It gets easier with practice, and he was already an expert, but the responsibility of that job can weigh on you. If I screwed up an IV placement —and I rarely screwed up an IV placement— the fluid we were putting in the patient's arm could leak out and damage the surrounding tissue. If Thomas made a mistake, the patient could asphyxiate or choke on his own blood or vomit. Thomas's eyes showed only concentration. He was a rock.

Andrew's skill was person-to-person therapy, usually in a quiet room. He was a psychiatric nurse, and a really good one at that, but today, he was in head-to-toe Personal Protective Equipment assessing patients as they came into our trauma bay, placing EKG leads, taking vital signs, and doing quick neurological assessments. He was the one who had to pronounce a patient dead before clearing the bay for a new one.

He was as methodical and as stoic as Thomas. I wondered what they were both really seeing when they looked at body after body coming into the bay. Perhaps they saw the severed limbs of our shipmates during our order's time in Malta, or the human offal in the trenches of the First

World War, or the severed heads of Saracen prisoners.

This was not even our first pandemic. We were well familiar with the chaos and suffering around us, but that didn't mean it didn't hurt. Our lives, our many lives, were often one trauma after another, just like this Emergency Department.

During one of these nightmares, Andrew lost his faith. It was during the Black Death in Italy. Once it was gone, he never looked back, and he never became a priest again. I don't know precisely when I lost my faith. There wasn't one moment where the realization landed on me, where I suddenly knew that I no longer believed. Now, though, it was well and truly gone.

Only Andrew paid attention to the clock, and this only because he needed an official time of death for each corpse. The rest of us ignored the clock. It was meaningless in trauma bay six; there was always another patient.

At some point in the long day, I wet myself. I could smell it in the suit, but I was way past caring. I suspected I wasn't the only one. We would all shower and put on street clothes before leaving, so I could just throw away my urine-soaked scrubs. We started each shift with a new set of PPE, but with dwindling supplies, that practice wouldn't last long.

We would run out soon, and once we started reusing things, I'd have to be more careful about peeing in my pants.

And then a woman was gently pushing me aside, taking the IV starting kit from me. I looked up to see four new nurses with marginally cleaner PPE. Our relief had arrived. I had no idea how long I had been on my feet, but when I made my way toward the locker room, I could only shuffle through the ankle-deep litter in the bay and, one hand against the wall, lumber down the hall and away from the Emergency Department, already half-asleep on my feet.

Three

All of the knights not currently roaming the Atlantic Ocean on a yacht shared an apartment in Violetville, only four blocks from Ascension St. Agnes Hospital, but I was so completely wiped out I took a cab. My head was full of cotton, so I didn't register that the young woman hugging me as I came through the door was Miranda, Aurora's girlfriend, whom I hadn't seen since just before the election, almost a year before.

I held her out at arm's length, getting a good look at her before pulling her into a longer hug.

"You look like death eating a graham cracker," she said, but I hushed her with a finger on my lips before leading her into the kitchen.

"We only talk in the kitchen. There's always somebody sleeping here," I said.

"So I see," she agreed. "Aurora is out like a light." She hooked her thumb toward one of the bedrooms.

"I assume you're sleeping there, too?" I asked, nodding to the room.

Miranda blushed. Kids.

"We moved into Simon's room."

"How did he feel about that?"

"He's staying with an ER doc downtown."

"We've only been here two weeks," I groaned.

"Simon's a hottie," she replied. "And I guess he works fast."

"That was *my* room too, you know," I whined. "Simon and I had to double up." The excitement at seeing Miranda wasn't holding my exhaustion at bay any longer.

Miranda touched her forehead to mine.

"Go to bed, Paul," she said and kissed me on the cheek. "There's a place in Augustine's room."

I woke up spooning Augustine, who was already awake and patiently waiting, so as not to disturb me. I tapped the back of her hand softly.

"Morning," I croaked.

"Evening," she corrected.

"How goes the plan to steal the world out of the arms of our enemy, general?"

"Not a clue. First order of battle is stay alive. We seem to be struggling even with that modest goal." After a pause she said, "It must be Easter."

"What? Easter isn't for another six months."

"He is risen," she replied looking back over her shoulder.

"That's just the early morning --you know," I said and pulled away from her back. She reached around and pulled me back to her.

"I know what it is," she said. She hooked her arm behind my head and stroked my hair. I closed my eyes and wanted to purr, but as I am an ancient and powerful knight sorcerer, I only sighed. That was enough encouragement. She moved my hand to her breast, and we made the beast with two backs as only two old friends can.

We emerged from the room showered and in fresh

scrubs to the smells of bacon and eggs cooking.

When you know you're going to be reincarnated, you don't worry much about saturated fats.

While Miranda cooked, Aurora stood, leaning on the refrigerator, looking at her phone. Augustine and I wrapped her up in an incredibly cheesy hug, which she bore with grace. She looked up at us when we let her go, and the corner of her mouth tugged up while she simultaneously raised one eyebrow.

"Did you two have some mommy-daddy time?" she asked.

Miranda snorted and ladled eggs onto plates.

"Do I ask you whether you've been munching your partner's carpet?" Augustine asked. The tone of her voice made me want to put on a sweater.

"Jesus Christ!" Aurora cried.

"Oh snap," Miranda murmured from the stove.

They all looked at me.

"A gentleman never tells."

This brought groans and much eye rolling.

The awkwardness was broken by Miranda placing breakfast on the table and filling our coffee cups.

"Beauty and smarts and she can cook, too," Augustine

said, hooking her chin toward Miranda.

I opened my mouth to add something when Aurora cut me off with a raised hand.

"I swear to God, Dad, if you say 'she's a keeper' I cannot be held responsible for my actions."

I smiled and took a long sip of coffee.

Discretion really is the better part of valor.

After an appropriate interval, during which I scarfed a dinner plate of scrambled eggs and eight pieces of bacon, I asked, "What's the situation at Hopkins?"

"It's the same everywhere," Aurora replied. "Most of them are dead before they get to us. The ones that make it are often brain damaged from the lack of oxygen. Hopkins had put out ads saying they're looking for anyone who has been bitten and survived. I guess they're working on treatments or maybe a vaccine."

"Did you give them your blood?" Augustine asked. The K-Nurses were immune to the illness that had already killed one-tenth of the world's population. We theorized that our time in the Ether had given us immunity so that we were not affected by the bite of Ether mosquitoes.

We had no data at all to support our theory, but the fact that vessels of the Returned were also immune gave it some credence.

The Ether mosquitoes had hitched a ride when Aurora returned from the Ether. Their saliva was so alien to the human body that it caused a massive allergic reaction, instant anaphylaxis.

"I didn't want to give blood without checking with you guys first," Aurora explained.

"I don't see any problem," I said. "There have been ordinary people who were asymptomatic."

Aurora nodded as Miranda sat down next to her.

We all looked at Miranda for a moment.

"How are you staying safe?" Augustine asked.

"I wear the netting and protective clothing when I'm outside and--" She paused, looking at Aurora.

"I've made a repellent spell for her," Aurora said. "I figure it costs me about ten minutes of life for every day I keep it going."

"A bargain at thrice the price," I said, and Miranda made a "go on" gesture. "But we should all take turns. You shouldn't bear the burden of that spell alone."

"Bart and Phil and I have the youngest bodies. We can handle it," she said, a tone of finality in her voice. "If they ever come back to land, they can help."

"We don't know if you'll be reborn," Augustine said. Every expenditure of magic makes me worry." She sighed. "I know you're an adult now. It's not my place to question."

Miranda placed her hand on Aurora's and looked at her. There was love and gratitude in that look, but also fear.

"James is having a really hard time," I said.

"And he shamelessly changes the subject," Miranda quipped.

Augustine turned to Miranda. "Paul is so smooth like that. He's right, though. Best not to dwell on my failures as a mother-substitute. Anyway, James is such a sensitive sort. I'm sure it's eating him up inside."

"We told him to take the day off, call in sick," said Thomas, who had slipped into the room without any of us realizing. He filled a tall, aluminum thermos cup with the last of the coffee before nodding to me. "Time to get going."

As I rose to follow him, I felt the tiniest pinch on my butt.

"I saw that!" Aurora shouted, her finger pointed in accusation.

"Shh," Augustine replied, unable to hide her grin. "You'll wake everyone up."

Four

 Some FEMA nurses had arrived overnight to help out, which gave us a full half-hour to eat. Thomas, Andrew, and I munched on the sandwiches Miranda had made for us, each of us lost in his private world. The room was well-enough soundproof that despite the chaos beyond the door, the only sound was the ticking of the big clock on the wall over the whiteboard and the drone of the TV high in the opposite corner.

 Thomas rose and moved to the TV to turn the volume up. In all of his incarnations, Thomas moves in a way that is somehow careful and bold at the same time. His current incarnation, a body the former occupant had allowed him to possess, was smaller than usual, and lighter-skinned, but despite his relatively diminutive size, he still generated a sense of power held in check.

". . . Last seen somewhere on the East Coast. They were reportedly working at a hospital in Florida, although only two of the terrorists had been caught on security camera footage," said the white woman with big blonde-white hair. A grainy, black-and-white picture appeared on the screen showing Andrew and Simon doffing their hoods and masks.

The camera moved to an energetic white man behind a desk, who was shaking his head. This was Al Windig, the Vice President. He was not one of the Returned, but no one endorsed their virulent racist theocracy harder than Windig. He was the kid in class whose hand was always as high as he could raise it. "Ooo, teacher! Pick me!" implied every time the hand went up.

That he was just an ordinary fascist was a sound strategic decision by Thaumiel/Roosevelt. Since Windig was a true believer, he would be a willing vessel for any of the Returned who needed a body. If Thaumiel was assassinated, he could simply enter Windig's body and continue on as president. Windig was essentially a spare body for Thaumiel.

"Anyone with information on the whereabouts of the

terrorists or their accomplices should call the number on your screen," said Windig, trying to inject some gravitas into his boyish demeanor. "As President Roosevelt says, 'If you see something, say something.' You don't have to be sure. The police will follow all leads, and together, we can cleanse America of these undesirables."

"Should we finish the shift?" Andrew asked.

I was too busy texting Aurora. *We're in a hurry to get to our next assignment*, I wrote. This meant that we should fly like Frodo from the Balrog.

Copy, was her reply, and I could hear the exhaustion and disappointment in that one word of text.

Thomas turned off the TV and stood under it, one hand on his hip, his head angled toward the floor, his eyes set in a thousand-yard-stare.

"We shouldn't risk it," Thomas said at last. "There were two guys in hoodies walking a block behind us this morning. I thought I was just paranoid, but they might have been the enemy. We'll need to change cars. Paul, find something in the lot big enough to carry gear. We'll probably need to get some on the way. Andrew, you should let Simon know."

"Already done," Andrew mumbled, looking at his phone.

Andrew and I went through the door with the current of Thomas's magic following us. We would all be wiped from the staffing logs and the memories of our coworkers. We took the elevator to the basement level, where we ditched our PPE and badges. Andrew found us maintenance staff coveralls in the locker room.

The parking lot was slim pickings. There was one white panel van that screamed SERIAL KILLER WITHIN, which seemed a poor choice when trying to maintain anonymity. We settled on an old Ford Flex. I laid my left hand on the driver's side door while pulling my right hand into a fist. When I opened it, a key fob and two keys lay against the palm. I opened the door on the other side with the fob, and Andrew jumped in, opening the glove box before he had fully landed and extracting the registration and insurance cards. He murmured a few words, then put them back.

"Changed the plates and registration?" I asked.

He nodded, and we were off.

We exited through the main gate, which was a serious tactical error. A throng of protesters blocked the road. They brandished signs accusing the hospital of being part of the "government scam." By which, I think they meant the pandemic. I saw two protesters go down, grabbing their throats, eyes bulging, but the rest of the crowd ignored them.

"Hard to believe this isn't magic at work," Andrew muttered. "People dropping like flies everywhere, and they still think it's a conspiracy."

"No one ever went broke underestimating the stupidity of the average terrified citizen."

"That's not the quote, you know."

"No bitterness here," I said, smirking.

I eased the car forward into the crowd. People pushed against the doors, banging on the window, so I put a mild electrical current into the doors. The banging stopped, and people moved back a step, and then I saw him. Gamaliel is pretty hard to miss. He is known as "the obscene one," and along with Lilith, he gave sex a bad name. He had possessed an enormous Sikh man in a dark blue caftan and turban. He grinned through a dark beard when his eyes met mine.

Before I could speak, Andrew's shield was up, pushing the crowd out of our way, but we weren't going faster than a run, and Gamaliel wasn't twenty meters behind. Andrew put his hands together in front of his chest and then pulled them apart, like Moses parting the Red Sea, and I gunned the engine as he did it. The crowd fell back to each side of our path.

We cleared the crowd and roared down Caton Ave, the back end sliding as we skidded left onto Benson. Andrew had one hand over his left ear while he shouted into his phone.

"Third rendezvous site!" he yelled.

Without slowing, I doubled-back, sliding onto Joh Street before running two red lights to get onto I-95 northbound.

"You couldn't take care of the lights?" I asked, unable to keep the annoyance out of my voice."

If I expected Andrew to get angry, I was sorely disappointed. He is our consigliere, our counselor and psychiatric nurse. He touched my shoulder.

"Warning the others was a higher priority." His voice was calm now that he didn't have to shout over the roaring of the engine. "They all pinged me back. We have groups going in four different directions. We should be at the rendezvous by noon tomorrow."

"Unless James changes it before then. OpSec and all that."

"I think not," he said. "James is struggling too much right now for his usual level of cyber security. This plague has really hit him hard. I haven't seen him like this since

Perpetua had to watch the English burn people alive."

Perpetua was James's female incarnation. He was sometimes born as a man, sometimes as a woman: James or Perpetua. James was the only one of us who was a woman in the original incarnation, our first lives, before we were murdered in Jerusalem. He had been a Spanish noblewoman and member of our order, but in order to wear armor and fight, she had to pretend to be a man. We all kept her secret.

James and Perpetua had been unaccepted in every incarnation. Perpetua was not allowed to bear arms without deception, and James wasn't manly enough to please the families that raised him. He was perhaps the most empathetic of us all, and given our lives of constant suffering and loss, the most withdrawn. He and Andrew had kept a special bond throughout the centuries. No one knew James better.

"Should we ditch the car now that Gamaliel has seen it?"

"Not yet," Andrew replied, sighing. "I have put a glamor on it. Let's leave that in place until we get to Tennessee."

"So what do we look like?"

"A Honda Civic."

"As good as camouflage."

Five

We arrived at the Gentleman Angler at four o'clock in the morning, just in time to see people, mostly men, loading their cars with gear and hooking up their boats. Pulaski, New York, a former industrial town on the shore of Lake Ontario, built its second-incarnation economy around fishing.

In the nineteenth century, a kind of invasive smelt, alewives, got into the lake. The population got so high that predators had to be introduced to control them. For some reason, the original native predators, Atlantic salmon, couldn't establish themselves, so Chinook and Coho salmon from the West Coast were introduced.

And a booming sport fishery was born to replace the failing mill economy.

The whole county was full of Roosevelt supporters, lots of guns and racist yard signs and billboards, but the business of Pulaski was fishing, so even a few medieval commies might find a place to rest, as long as they were seen to have the trappings of a fisher. We were hiding out right under the enemy's nose.

The Gentleman Angler was a hotel uniquely built to serve the needs of its fishing patrons. The rooms were more like bunkhouses than traditional hotel rooms. Each room had an antechamber for hanging waders, and the communal living room had rows of benches for tying flies.

Simon, James, Aurora, and Miranda were huddled around a table in the middle of the room when Andrew and I slunk in.

"Ridden hard and put away wet," said Simon, looking us up and down.

"Where's Augustine?" Andrew asked.

"She's on a call with Peter and the twins," Aurora replied. "They think the boat has been spotted in port, and they're deciding how to deal with it."

Augustine was our general. She had to approve any proposed changes in strategy. Peter, Bart, and Phil had stayed aboard a yacht that was our mobile command center. We had all fled there when our headquarters in South Carolina was attacked, but only these three had stayed on the ship after the pandemic began.

We thought it would be safe in international waters off the coast of Africa, but every boat has to put in at some point for gas and supplies. The most convenient port was Las Palmas in the Canary Islands. Since the election that put Garridan Roosevelt in the White House, proto-fascist, neo-fascist, and just old-fashioned fascist movements had been on the rise in Europe.

In Spain, this took the form of a rewriting of history around the rule of Generalissimo Franco, the dictator who governed the country from the 1930's to the 1970's.

Franco had been in a kind of exile in Las Palmas before the Spanish Civil War, so it was not surprising that his particular brand of homicidal madness might find a foothold there.

Augustine and the boat-dwellers were plotting how to disguise the appearance of the ship, change the name on the hull, the flag, anything that could be changed, but with a ship that size, they wouldn't be able to do much. Adding insult to injury, our new living quarters were so small that Augustine had to make the call on a satellite phone in a shed used for cleaning fish behind the hotel.

There were nine beds in our room, three sets of three bunks, each with identical sheets and woolen blankets. It wasn't too far from an army barracks or a prison, but people *paid* to stay there. On the bottom, unoccupied bunk along the east wall of the room was a pile of fishing equipment, most with price tags still on, and an assortment of firearms. Unlike the fishing tackle, the firearms were not new.

Simon waved toward a set of deep shelves with a TV and a coffee maker on top. I offered Andrew a cup, but he shook his head, so I filled a mug and joined the group.

In the center of the table was a laminated map of the eastern United States. It was covered in erasable marker notes and symbols.

"The Left Hand of God is active again." Simon indicated blue marks up and down the coast and some as far west as Iowa.

"Augustine must be thrilled," I moaned. "I thought we cut off their funding."

"They have plenty of donors since Roosevelt took

office," Miranda said. She looked at me and seemed to be avoiding Aurora.

"I think we have to be careful of the Left Hand," Aurora grumbled. "At bottom, they're just a bunch of thugs."

"But they're *our* thugs," Miranda said. "They want the same things we want. They're fighting for the same cause we are."

Miranda scanned the table, gauging everyone's reaction, everyone except Aurora.

Simon had always supported the Left Hand. "You don't have to convince me," he said, looking at Aurora.

"We are not having this argument again," Aurora grumbled.

"What argument?" Augustine asked as she came through the door.

"Left Hand of God," Aurora said.

"Again? We are spending far too much time on this issue."

Miranda stood up, calming herself as she rose, and walked out the door. She might have slammed it a little.

Andrew watched everyone, no doubt assessing the emotional state of everyone in the room. His voice was surprising in the silence that followed Miranda's exit; most of us had forgotten he was there.

"How long has this been an issue?" he asked.

"Miranda wants to join the Left Hand," Augustine answered. "I think she's misguided, but she's a grown woman."

"She's behaving like a child," Aurora spat.

"Disagreeing with you doesn't mean she's being childish," Andrew replied. "It must be intimidating, not to mention invalidating, to be the only civilian in a group of sorcerer knights."

"She's known how it is since the beginning," Aurora replied, her voice softening as if she realized mid-sentence how defensive she was being. This kind of insight, this was Andrew's unique magic.

"What news from sea?" I asked, pointedly rerouting the conversation.

Augustine's lips drew into a thin line, her eyebrows meeting above her nose.

"Peter thinks they were identified while the boat was in port. There have been flyovers by military jets, high altitude, followed by lower surveillance flights by drones. He really needs James to cook up some counter measures."

James was doodling in a little puddle of spilled coffee in

front of him. He didn't look up, even when his name was mentioned. He flicked a finger and suddenly a newscaster's voice rumbled loudly in the room. I don't know where he got the broadcast from, but I guessed the communal living room.

"The public is asked to forward any information concerning the fugitives to their local Office of Homeland Security. These men and women are considered armed and extremely dangerous. Do not approach them."

Six

Under cover of darkness, I helped Miranda bring our groceries into the Gentleman Angler. She did the shopping because she was the only one of us whose face wasn't all over the news. She found a twenty-four-hour grocery store and purchased supplies just before midnight.

I say supplies. It was more like two bags of frozen meals and some oranges that must have had several stamps on their passports. Our room being a fishing retreat, we had a decent sized freezer and a microwave.

"That took a while," Aurora said without looking up

from her tablet.

Miranda closed her eyes, hands on hips, and exhaled.

"Long lines this time of night at the checkout?" Aurora doubled down on the snark.

"How am I supposed to talk to you about this stuff if you treat me this way?" Miranda replied in a tone that would have made any sensible person careful about proceeding.

My daughter is not always sensible.

"So you did meet with them. You met with the Left Hand." Aurora said it as a statement of fact.

"They are out there fighting!" Miranda cried, whirling on Aurora. "They're not holed up in some dump playing possum. They're actually *doing something*."

Andrew swung his legs over the top bunk and jumped to the floor.

"Terrorism is terrorism," said Augustine from her bed.

"It's *counter*-terrorism!" Miranda shouted.

"I'm glad you're getting involved," said Andrew, "but random acts of violence don't make for a winning strategy."

"How are we supposed to coordinate our efforts if you won't even talk to them?" asked Simon, stepping out of the bathroom in a white terrycloth robe.

"They sabotaged the Air Guard base near Syracuse,"

murmured James. "Two planes lost, seven airmen injured."

Aurora's eyes widened and her head swung toward Miranda.

"We were after the planes. The soldiers or whatever were collateral damage. We're deep in Roosevelt country here," Miranda said, defiant. "We needed to send a message."

I wanted to send Miranda to her room, but there were several problems with that plan: 1) she was a grown woman, 2) I was not her father, 3) we were all standing in the middle of her room, and 4) I'm not entirely sure she wasn't right, about the planes at least.

Aurora's face betrayed bald disgust and contempt.

I don't have Andrew's insight into the workings of the heart, but disgust and contempt didn't seem like good emotions to inject into an intimate relationship.

"Your food's here. I'm going to get my own room," Miranda said, challenging Aurora to argue. Aurora said nothing. She sat back in her chair and folded her arms.

"Will you be safe?" James asked, his soft voice slicing the silence.

"Good point," Miranda replied. She went to the bottom bunk with the weapons cache, selected a nine millimeter pistol —I think it was my CZ 75 SP-01. I really like that gun, so I was a little conflicted about giving it to her— chambered a round, stuck it in the small of her back under the waistband and stormed out. This time she did not slam the door, which made it worse.

Aurora snorted, then choked, her eyes welling, then she slammed her hand on the table, and her tears disappeared.

Augustine sighed.

"She's right that we can't keep retreating. With all of our faces on TV every day, Roosevelt's got us boxed in. If they capture the command center, too, we'll really be in trouble," she said.

"Peter doesn't need me," James practically whispered. "Bart and Phil know more about boats and planes than I ever will. I'm sure they've got this covered."

"That's not how Peter felt," Augustine replied.

"Peter has never given them much credit."

With that, James shuffled to his bed, the bottom bunk under Andrew and Simon, slid under the blanket, and turned toward the wall.

"The Left Hand is much bigger than its previous form," Simon began. "They've got chapters on both coasts and some in the Rust Belt. They're too big an ally to ignore.

Remember the Siege of Malta? Sure, that Italian prince took his sweet time, but in the end, he came through with reinforcements. If we had just written him off as unreliable, we would have lost the whole island."

"I was already dead by the time reinforcements arrived," I reminded him. "So was Jude." His name brought the conversation to a crashing halt.

"So?" Simon hissed. "Who cares if that pig-fucker was dead before the reinforcements arrived? We should never have banished him. I'd want to awaken him in every incarnation so that I could cut his fucking throat another time. Or burn him alive over and over."

"I see why you like the Left Hand of God so much," Augustine quipped.

"Fuck you."

"Entertaining as this is," I said, "it doesn't get us any closer to a plan. Unless we can send some of the top Returned execs back to the Ether, we're going to be on the run through this lifetime and those to come. We have to stop them before they accumulate even more power."

"We may be too late," Augustine said. "It seems the gateway between the worlds has opened more. Cogs are possessing ordinary people, but not in the numbers I would have thought."

"Beast is keeping them busy," Aurora said with obvious satisfaction."

B-E7-10, or "Beast" to his friends, was a cog that Aurora had given magic. We believed he was leading a revolution against the Returned back in the Ether. Because they had to fight a rearguard action there, they couldn't send all of their heavy hitters to our world. Lilith hadn't been seen for weeks.

"You think he's convincing cogs to stay in the Ether?" I asked, incredulous.

Aurora nodded. I just scratched my head. It would be silly to count on this being true, but it was a ray of hope at a very dark time.

"It kills me to agree with Simon," Augustine said, "but I think he's right; we have to bring the fight to them."

"And work with the Left Hand of God?" Aurora shouted, rising.

"I'm afraid so."

Seven

The big motors of the boat chugged slowly through the chop of the lake, like racehorses held back to a walk. Long thin metal arms extended out each side of the boat, outriggers they were apparently called. The hooks on the end of the lines that ran through the outriggers were not baited. Like everything else about this fishing trip, they were just for show.

The captain and mate were both members of the Left Hand of God. The group had been around for years, but had been mostly based in the Carolinas, and mostly funded by our council. Shortly before the assassination of Prentiss

Gilchrist, Garridan Roosevelt's predecessor, we had withdrawn their funding. Most of the council agreed that they had become too extreme and too indiscreet: they had taken to nailing members of the KKK to flaming crosses.

The Left Hand had its champions on the council, though, most notably Simon, and to a lesser degree, Thomas. The two of them were huddled in the cabin of the boat with the mate, Ann Mitchel, going over a map. I was here as a neutral third party, which had made Aurora apoplectic. I had started to wonder whether she was more upset about the Left Hand or the fact that her girlfriend had joined up.

High above the boat, in a powder blue sky, just under the cotton ball clouds, a drone made its lazy way back and forth across the lake. It looked like a grid search pattern to me, so I climbed the short ladder to the little bridge where the captain had already taken out binoculars.

"Any markings?"

"Negative," he replied. "We should probably catch a fish or two, though. We're trolling through an area with a lot of fish. If we don't pull any in, it will look suspicious. Keep her pointed so that we stay even with the shore." He said, stepping aside so that I could take the helm.

"What does that stuff do?" I asked, indicating the array

of switches on the dashboard in front of me.

"I will cut off your fingers if you touch them. So don't touch them. Don't touch anything."

"Except the wheel."

"Except that."

"Aye, aye," I said.

He sneered and looked like he wanted to say more, but instead, backed over the ladder and slid to the deck.

I had commanded a ship many times the size of this fishing boat, and a crew of thirty corsairs. In those days, I might have blustered at him, or literally rattled my sword. He was the captain, though, so I obeyed. The boat didn't require much steering; it moved in a straight line all on its own. Then I noticed that the wheel was locked in place. He had me up here pretending to steer so that I would stay out of his way while he baited our lines.

That was hurtful.

Not ten minutes after he had put on the lures, he yelled "fish on!"

Simon stepped out of the cabin and the captain handed him a rod. Simon pumped the rod up and down, reeling intermittently until the captain reached out with a long-handled net and scooped up a nice King Salmon. It was a male with a hooked jaw and slashes of pink along the gill plates. The drone hovered above, just off our port side. When Simon held the fish up, it rose and resumed its search grid.

The captain gaffed the fish and put it in a cooler set into the deck.

"That's a Fish and Wildlife drone," he said. "They're taking a survey for fishing reports on the east side of the lake."

"That will feed us for a couple of nights," Thomas said, stretching as he emerged from the cabin."

"I'd be careful about eating those," Ann said. "There's a lot of pollution in the lake."

We chuckled.

"We have strong immune systems," Thomas explained. "Will drones like that get in the way of the raid? We don't want an accidental sighting to turn the whole operation pear-shaped."

"They don't fly them at night," Ann said. The captain shook his head in agreement.

"Coast Guard will be a bigger problem," he said. "And local law enforcement. Including the unofficials."

Thomas saw my confusion.

"Local yahoos with guns who want to play shoot-em-up," he explained.

The captain nodded at a fishing rod with a deep bend on the starboard side, and Ann went to reel it in.

"Four teams," the captain said. "Two to create diversions at Oswego and Rochester Border Patrol stations with one team in reserve. The main strike will be Homeland Security in Batavia"

"James has already finished the virus, but we have to get it into the network," said Simon.

"The easy part," I added.

"You trust this guy making the virus?"

Simon, Thomas, and I glared at him. Simon broke first and giggled.

"He has no peer in this kind of thing," I said. "Once the virus is uploaded, it will destroy Homeland Security's database, starting with citizens of interest."

"The American Gestapo," Thomas muttered.

"And you trust the guy on the inside?" I asked, only partially because I was annoyed that he asked about James. I'm petty like that.

"Woman on the inside," said Ann, throwing a long, slender salmon into the cooler. She saw us staring at it.

"Coho," she said, by way of explanation.

"No body count this time," Thomas warned.

The captain shrugged.

"We don't all have the same mojo you guys do. We'll do what we have to do to keep our people safe."

"We aren't going to win hearts and minds with another massacre like the Air Guard raid," I said.

He fixed me with a stare that was supposed to turn my knees to water. Five hundred years back, I would have cut off one of his ears just for looking at me like that, but I like to think I've matured a little vis-à-vis lopping off body parts. I still didn't like getting the SNEER OF DEATH from this punk.

"You do you," I said, and shot him with my index finger.

Eight

The Department of Homeland Security office in Batavia sits across a pond from the county sheriff's office and is surrounded by cheap motels. You would never know it was an important government data hub . . . except for the twenty-foot high chain link fence with razor wire and the spotlights and signs that read, KEEP OUT, TRESPASSERS MAY BE SHOT. I found a little hope in the sign's use of the subjunctive; I was that desperate for something encouraging. Except for the fence, etc., though, totally discrete.

I was more than a little leery about the information we

had on the cite. It had all come from Left Hand sources, and I remained a skeptic despite Augustine's frequent assurances. At this point, it was way too late to complain.

Aurora and Augustine were in the group that would lead the diversion at Rochester Border Patrol, while Simon and Thomas led the group at Oswego. James and I were to infiltrate the Batavia Office of Homeland Security and plant the computer virus. Miranda was in the reserve group which was made up entirely of members of the Left Hand.

If all went to plan at 00:13, Group 1 would cut the power to the buildings in Rochester, which should sound an alarm and put the whole station on alert. At 00:30, Group 2 would break into the Oswego office and set off as many alarms as possible. The idea was to draw the lion's share of law enforcement to these two stations. While they were all looking toward Border Patrol, James and I would magic our way into the Homeland Security office.

That was the plan, anyway. As I've said before, no plan survives contact with the enemy. It had been a long time since I was part of a plan that had gone so wrong. But I didn't find out the full extent of it until the next day.

James cloaked us and coaxed the door open. He had gotten a picture of a name badge, just a picture, and had duplicated it on his left hand. He got us through door after door by just holding up his hand. It was all very Star Wars.

The elevator was immaculate, military clean and shiny, and the panel showed three underground levels. We went to the lowest one first. The door opened onto a dimly lit room of shelves and racks. Most of it was personnel equipment: vests, battering rams, com units, and the like. There was no sign of any computer equipment. We searched all four walls for another door or hallway. Nothing.

James closed his eyes and leaned against the concrete wall. He had lost so much weight that his eyes were sunken. When he closed them, he looked corpse-like. He startled me when his eyes flew open.

"I can hear the hum of the servers, so they're probably right above us."

"Back to the elevator, then?"

"There's a ladder on the south wall that looks like it goes to a maintenance hatch. Let's take a look first. Coming through the front door makes me uneasy."

"Okey dokey," I said.

James smiled.

Like the elevator, the stairway and maintenance hatch were clean as a whistle. The ceiling was too low to stand fully, so we crawled on hands and knees to a duct where a waterfall of cables entered the maintenance space from the floor above.

"Do the finger thing," I pleaded.

James sighed.

"Come on. It's really cool."

"You are a child," James whispered. Nonetheless, he laid his right hand along the bundle of cables and closed his eyes. His fingers extended up through the duct. He held his left hand up, palm forward, and four different views were projected on the wall, one from each finger.

"So cool," I started to say, but what I saw shut me up. A phalanx of men in body armor with Kevlar shields were poised, automatic weapons raised, pointing toward the elevator door. Behind the men, in a sharkskin suit, Samael looked at his nails.

A walkie-talkie crackled above us, and I heard one of the soldiers say, "They're in the building. We're waiting for them on L2. Yes, sir, as soon as we know."

"We've been rumbled. Again," I said.

James wasn't looking at me. He was so deep in thought that his pupils moved rapidly back and forth. I extended my senses in three dimensions and felt subtle traces of magic all around us. Samael wasn't the only Returned in the building.

"Their magic is looking for us," James said. "It's only a matter of time."

"We can't break through a wall; we're forty meters underground."

"The only way out is up," he agreed.

"Slither?"

"I'm afraid so."

Fear of serpents is a natural human reflex, hard-wired. That's my story, and I'm sticking to it. Apologies to the reptile lovers of the world, but seriously? The only thing worse than touching a snake is becoming one, but it was one way to get through really tight spaces. Although I am a dedicated atheist, the old training never quite goes away: I know it's superstitious to associate snakes with evil, but I do.

"I'll get their attention first," I said, extending my mind toward the elevator. I had to visualize the panel in order to push the right button, but I knew I'd gotten it right when the door dinged and a cacophony of gunfire erupted above me.

Then I was feeling the metal and plastic of the cable bundle, my scales grasping their surface, my smooth body moving upward. I could see the area immediately around me, but not much further. My tongue was the first to sense emergence onto the floor of Level 2. The temperature was colder, and I moved quickly away from the scent of cordite. I could feel the uneven pulsing of the floor with all the shooting, and I moved to a warmer space under a stack of servers. I couldn't see snake-James behind me.

Men screamed and debris flew all around me as a great spinning wind flung everyone and everything over the big room. I could make out shapes of people and things flying around, but I couldn't see any detail. At least the shooting had stopped.

I slithered out from under the server rack, transformed back into myself, and immediately started coughing. My eyes blurred with tears, and I had to drop to the ground again to get a breath.

The room was on fire.

Nine

Despite my immediate alarm at the smoke and flames, my mind went instantly to the other teams where my brothers and sister --and more importantly, my daughter-- were likely also walking into traps. The leak must have been in the Left Hand of God. It could have been Jude; he had a talent for guessing our next move. While it was possible, the more likely scenario was that someone in the Left Hand was a double agent.

I couldn't see James anywhere as I crawled, first on my knees, then on my belly, toward the emergency exit. The fire door had kept the smoke out of the stairway, and my ears rang from the change in pressure. It took me a moment to clear them and take in the surrounding stairway. If the enemy lay in wait, I was done for.

Mercifully, they were not there. In fact, the stairway was quiet and brightly lit, the only sound the crackling of flames on the other side of the door. Someone must have disabled the fire alarms. I ascended slowly, checking every turn. My boots rang on the metal steps and echoed up and down the stairway shaft. I went past the first floor stairway door, keeping low. I figured if anyone was waiting, it would be on the ground floor.

A quick glance through the mesh-reinforced window told me I was right. I darkened the space immediately behind the window with magic, making it like one-way glass so that I could get a better look at the room. James was unconscious, slung over some ape's shoulder as he trundled toward the front door. I began to marshal my will when I felt two energies, one on the other side of the door, the other back in the burning server room. They were searching for me, so I turned off all of my magic and moved as quietly as I could to the top of the stairway, emerging onto the roof through a locked door that was easily opened with picks, not magic.

I emerged onto the roof in time to see a hospital helicopter rise in front of me, the propeller wash showering me with debris. The copter tilted and headed toward the lake. Once it was out of sight, I called a gull that had been hovering above me and told her to find our reserve unit on the lake and bring them as close as possible. She flew off in the right direction, but gulls have their own agenda. They are not as dependable as pigeons or even ravens or crows. I made it even odds that she would deliver my message.

Three black Escalades and a brown van drove single file out the front gate, leaving armed guards at intervals along the fence and the driveway. Nobody was going in or out after those cars.

At moments like these I have time to contemplate my own immortality. The horrors of my past lives pass before my eyes, and the prospect that I will never have peace puts me in a really bad mood. I get cranky, and when I'm cranky, I do some of my best magic. I decided to take a page from the Returneds' own playbook; I was going to illusion the shit out of this place.

Above the front door, the night skies parted, and a beam of bright light shone from the heavens. Descending on a cloud were Aurora, Augustine, and Perpetua, James's female form, last incarnated in mid-nineteenth century England. They were dressed in white togas, and Augustine raised a golden lightning bolt in one hand as they neared the ground.

In centuries past, illusions would have been of angels or demons. Today, I used a format the knuckle-draggers in black would hold in highest regard: a Hollywood Blockbuster.

Before the cloud had landed on the ground, gunfire rained on the illusion from every angle. I did not take any time to admire my handiwork, instead beating feet back into the building and out the first floor fire door.

They had forgotten to turn the alarms back on, so despite the ALARM WILL SOUND sticker, I went through silently. A thunderous crash behind me told me the illusion was coming to an end. Illusion-Augustine had flung her thunderbolt. It had exploded and made the ground shake.

In Surround Sound.

I sliced through the back fence with a spell and was into the pond before the clouds of gun smoke had cleared in the front of the building. Glass was still clinking from the plate windows in the front. They were bulletproof, but nothing will repel thousands of rounds at once.

I heard, but did not see, the returning helicopter, as I

was at the bottom of the pond. I stayed there for more than an hour after the sounds outside settled. No sirens, no more shots, nothing, just the sounds of an urban green space, the odd frog, crickets, distant traffic sounds. I still had plenty of air in the bubble I had taken with me, but I was too agitated to wait. James had been taken, and I needed to know if any of the other knights were still alive.

I sloshed out of the water to a waiting gull. She was standing remarkably still, not hopping around like they usually do. This was a serious bird. She walked calmly to me, and as I bent down to her, I heard Augustine's voice coming from the bird's beak.

"State park on the lake. Cabin 6."

I nodded to the gull, who dipped her beak once before rising into the air and sailing on the wind toward the lake.

This is where I wish I could tell you I turned into an eagle and soared off, or that I ran at 200 kilometers per hour, a human bullet train, or that I invented some other way of making a heroic exit. But with all the magic I had used and losing James, I was so exhausted I just called an Uber.

Ten

Selkirk Shores is a sprawling campground and beach right on the shore of Lake Ontario. There were hookups for campers, tent sites, and a dozen or so rustic cabins. We had moved to one of the cabins, and the crew was sprawled over every piece of furniture when I got there. It made the Gentleman Angler look luxurious.

Thomas had a bandage over his left eye that was seeping blood. Aurora's arm was wrapped from shoulder to wrist, and Simon was wearing a dress. Just another Tuesday for the K-Nurses.

"Where's Andrew?" I asked, dropping my waterlogged

boots on the door mat.

"He's sleeping," Augustine said. She had a tray with four steaming mugs, which she set down on the rough plank table. "He got the worst of it."

I surveyed the room again, this time noticing three neat stitches on Augustine's cheek.

"They knew we were coming," Simon said, his voice clipped. "They were set up for an ambush, so they had plenty of advance notice."

"What's with the dress?" I asked Simon. "That shade of yellow really doesn't work for you."

"He had to flame up to get us out of there, and this was all I had," Augustine answered for him.

I wanted to be glib, to say, "work it, work it" or make some other joke, anything to break the horrible tension that gripped the room, but between the somber mood and the news I had to deliver about James, I just couldn't.

"This wasn't Jude," I observed. All the heads in the room dipped as if in prayer, except Aurora."

"This leak came from the Left Hand," Aurora said, eyes bright either with tears or anger.

"Speaking of which, where is Miranda?"

"We don't know," Augustine responded. "The whole

reserve unit is missing. We lost contact with them just before the raid. If the enemy was ready for us, I can only assume it was pretty bad for you too. Sending the gull was weird, but creative. I'll give you that."

I opened my mouth to speak, but the memory of James slung over a back like a sack of potatoes made the words catch in my throat. I closed my eyes, laid my palm on my chest, and breathed. When I opened my eyes, everyone was looking at me.

"They got James," I said at last.

"Is he dead?" Thomas asked.

"I don't think so. He was unconscious but still breathing, I think, when they took him out of the building. They had a whole company of security, and two of the Returned were there. I was just lucky they didn't get me as well."

Thomas's face became a mask. "Any clue about where they're taking him?"

I shook my head.

Tears were running down Aurora's cheeks, but she did not sob or cry out. It was as if she didn't know she was crying.

Augustine broke the silence. "We think it was the fishing

boat's captain. He insisted that the reserve crew not have anyone other than Left Hand people, no knights. My guess is that he's a thousand miles from here by now."

Thomas moved like light and flung the door open, and Miranda tumbled in. Her face was bruised all along the right side, and she had wrapped a piece of cloth around the palm of her left hand. She landed on her knees and swayed for a moment before rising with a groan. Aurora never moved or said a word.

"He's not a thousand miles away," Miranda began. "I buried him about half a mile down the shoreline. They'll find him in the spring when the water rises."

She fell into a wooden chair next to the table and didn't seem to notice when Augustine unwrapped her hand.

"The captain and mate from our fishing trip, they were the ones. They took me out on the lake in the reserve group to use me as leverage, in case any of you made it out. And they talked. A lot. They planned to kill me if they didn't need me as a hostage, so I killed them first."

"All three of them?" Simon asked.

Miranda's jaw tightened. She looked directly into Aurora's eyes before answering.

"Figuring how to drive the boat back was harder."

Aurora's tears flowed again, filling her eyes and overrunning the lids. The fat tears made soft plops on the map in front of her.

"According to those guys," Miranda explained, "the Left Hand of God is riddled with spies from Homeland Security. There's a special unit run by 'two really scary guys.'"

Thomas and I looked at each other.

"Samael was there for sure," I said. "I could feel someone else, but I couldn't be sure who it was."

"Ghagiel," Thomas and Simon said together.

"When you don't know who, it's that bastard," Thomas added.

"My nemesis," Augustine said. "My problem."

Thomas raised an eyebrow.

"We don't have the personnel for vendettas, I know," Augustine replied, "but if I get a shot at him . . ." She trailed off.

"We need our general now," I implored her, "not a cage fighter."

Aurora wobbled as she got to her feet.

"We know there was a traitor. Are we just going to take her word for it? For who turned us in?" She pointed toward Miranda. "How likely is it that she killed three men herself?"

Miranda rose.

"You can't be serious," she barked. "You think *I* betrayed you?"

"Let's all calm down," Augustine pleaded. "This has been a difficult day for everyone."

"She doesn't seem all that broken up about killing three people," Aurora accused. "Look at her!"

"You know those aren't my first," Miranda said, knocking her chair over as she spun. "I didn't see you bawling after you killed Gilchrist. Why should I fall apart now? You think I'm so frail." She stomped toward the door, turning just as she grabbed the handle. "Who *are* you?" she hissed at Aurora before rushing out into the darkness and the drizzle.

I watched her through the open door, running toward the lake.

"What is she talking about?" Thomas demanded, rounding on Aurora.

She sagged onto her outstretched arms.

"While I was away, the Returned sent some flunkie to get her, take her hostage. They wanted her because I was being uncooperative."

Was she ever.

"Miranda killed him, sent him back to the Ether. It broke something in her. She had never killed anything before. She made me swear I would never tell anyone. She thought you guys would banish her or something because she was a murderer."

I don't know how long Andrew had been standing in the doorway to his bedroom. He was like Thomas in his ability to move quietly.

"She had to kill to avoid becoming a hostage," he said. "It's not surprising she might go postal on the guys who tried to do it again tonight. Maybe she doesn't want us to see her as a liability. Maybe she wants to fight for her love."

Aurora's head tilted to Andrew.

"Or maybe she made the whole thing up," she said.

"You don't believe that, and neither do I."

Eleven

Three weeks later, we were in a small town outside Salt Lake City. Getting our fake identities and nursing credentials without James was harder than any of us remembered. For all our lifetimes of experience we were all pretty stupid when it came to the digital world.

That wasn't the only reason we missed James so badly. We had all been taken prisoner at one time or another. I actually died of dysentery in a French prison during the Napoleonic Wars. This time was different, though. We needed all of the knights to have any chance of reversing the tide from the Ether, and we had all noticed how James, always an introvert, had given up at the end. He had withdrawn so deeply that he was a stranger even to Andrew.

James was a sweet and caring soul who had to stay away from bedside nursing because he was too empathetic. Twice, once as James and once as Perpetua, he was so desperate to stop the suffering around him that he used up his whole life in a week of curing magic. The first time was during the Black Death. He saved thousands and aged seventy years in seven days.

Our grief and loss at his capture had not yet turned to anger, but it soon would.

St. Ignatius of the Mountains was small compared to other hospitals in the area, with less than a hundred beds. Thomas and Simon worked nights in the ED, and the rest of us worked on a unit that cared for patients with hypoxic brain injuries from the pandemic. These poor souls had survived, or rather, been resuscitated, but had endured a period without oxygen to their brains. They had a whole spectrum of troubles from speaking to walking, to behaviors like tics and chorea, to paranoia and delusion.

To keep from being recognized, we had to use a glamor to hide our faces under a kind of movable mask, like magic make-up that moved with our faces. It was the only way to keep from being recognized; our faces were on the news almost every day.

The glamor worked, but, like all magic, it cost us life. We couldn't afford to keep doing it, but we agreed that we had to be taking care of patients during the pandemic, even if it cost us.

On the upside, we didn't have to wear hazmat suits in the hospital. Engineers had effectively closed the hospital to anything bigger than viruses, and all of the doorways had high pressure airlocks to keep bugs out. The hallways had bug zappers every five meters, and environmental services workers applied repellent to the windows daily.

While I had to give the hospital high marks for protecting the patients and staff within its walls, they had utterly lost the public relations war in their community.

To wit, a band of protesters by each hospital entrance proclaiming the pandemic was a sham, and that prevention was a waste of taxpayer dollars. The CDC had recommended repellent and the wearing of beekeeping gear: the helmet, face net, and thick gloves. Stores had sold out of them in three days, and now the industry was ramping up production. Head nets and gloves now sold for almost $1000 if you could find them.

The protesters, of course, did not wear any protection, although I swear I could smell repellent on some. Ironically, my immunity to the mosquitoes from the Ether allowed me to walk right through the protesters; I wasn't wearing protective gear either, so they thought I was a like-minded zealot.

On my way to and from work every day, I saw people in the mob fall over and suffocate while their fellows ignored them. This really brought the power of the moment home to me. People were watching the effects, seeing others die right in front of them, and refusing to accept the cause.

The human mind can be a remarkable dumpster fire.

Inside, on my unit, I cared for the casualties. One young man, perhaps in his mid-thirties, was so confused that he became dangerous when frustrated. He was six-four and a solid two hundred forty pounds. He had long, curly hair and an equally long unkempt beard, and he was really angry most of the time.

The night shift had put him in leather restraints —I don't even want to think about how many people that took— and in his thrashing, he had severed the headboard and footboard from the hospital bed. He was tied to the bed frame, his ankles and wrists locked in heavy leather manacles.

By the time I came on duty, he had calmed down. He looked around the room, obviously confused, as if waking up in a strange place, and tugged half-heartedly at the restraints. Hospital policy required us to loosen the restraints every two hours to make sure that the patient hadn't hurt themselves. It was obvious from the welts under his wrists that this hadn't been done. I wanted to say something about it, but that wouldn't have been fair. I was a trained soldier, and I had magic. Loosening the restraints for anyone else would have been incredibly dangerous.

"Morning, buddy," I said, raising the shade. "Tough night, huh?"

"Tommy?"

There was such pleading in his face, I couldn't bear to correct him.

"It's me."

"Why, Tommy? Why would you take Gloria away from me? You did me dirty, man."

"It wasn't like that. I didn't take Gloria. It was just a dream."

"But it felt so real, Tommy. I was right there."

He started to cry. I knelt beside the bed and put my forehead against his. He tried to hug me, but the restraints stopped him, so I untied them all, and we sat on the bed in a tight embrace while he sobbed. He kept saying "Tommy, Tommy" over and over, and all I could think to do was hold him.

Twelve

Aurora and I sat on an octagonal bench in a city park, baseball diamonds in every direction, and ate sushi from a restaurant up the street. No one was playing or practicing at this time of day in December, and Salt Lake City was surprisingly devoid of snow. The mountains that surrounded the city were famous for their snowfall, some of the highest in the West, even with global climate change. But the city was dry and brown and warm.

I was a late-comer to sushi, although I had eaten ceviche through many lives. Aurora had always liked sushi, though. She had introduced me to the variety of raw fish dishes, and

I had become a devotee. Now, though, she sat next to me on the bench and picked at her food. She wouldn't meet my eyes.

I've been a father for less time than I have been anything else. Even though my daughter was a grown woman, I still felt like a newbie at the parenting thing, and I was less confident in my ability to wing it than Augustine, to whom mothering had come naturally. By trial and error I had found out that sometimes it's best to be quiet, and sometimes it's best to get the conversation started.

I had no clue which this was, so I was quiet, because it was easier and less likely to get me in trouble or to hurt her.

Eventually my patience paid off. She sighed, set her food aside, and looked into the distance.

"It's like I don't even know her anymore."

"Because of the Left Hand?"

"Not just that. She's changed. She's not the sweet funny woman I knew."

"It's a tough time for sweet and funny. You've been raised thinking you might escape the real death, that you might never lose the people you love most. She has always lived with the knowledge that some day, her time will be up. You can't know what it did to her to be confronted with that so violently," I said before popping a piece of tuna roll in my mouth.

"I know, but, you know, not her. It shouldn't happen to her."

I finished chewing. I made myself go slow because I was way too invested in the next moment.

"So you tried to protect her from entering the dangerous world that is your calling?"

"Exactly," Aurora replied, tilting her head and raising an eyebrow."

"And when you tried to protect her by making decisions for her, she resented it and pushed you away?"

Aurora put her hands on her thighs and cracked her neck. Her mouth lifted into a half smile, but it was sad just the same.

"How long have you been waiting to say that?"

"About ten years," I said. I wasn't gloating, not outwardly, anyway. Aurora, though, is really smart, and really smart daughters are trouble.

"Rather than give you the satisfaction of seeing me struggling with the same grief I put you through, let's use your experience to help me."

I should be a big enough man to have accepted that with

grace, but truth be told, I was a little disappointed. I had a whole rant prepared about all of the times she had scared the bejesus out of me when she was growing up and training to be a knight. My disappointment showed on my face.

Aurora smirked.

"How did you do it? How did you deal with the fear? She's only been training for a few weeks, and she's already going on dangerous assignments."

"Your first mission was the assassination of a public figure," I pointed out.

"But I had been training for *years*."

"And you have magic."

"True that," she chimed in. "But she doesn't."

"It sounds like her near abduction was the experience that set all this in motion," I said. "This was her awakening rite. It's completely understandable."

She groaned and kicked at the dirt.

"I dealt with it by encouraging your training and trusting in my brothers and sister," I continued. "I figured if I couldn't talk you out of it, I should make sure you were as tough and smart about combat as you could be."

"And nursing."

"And nursing too. I had to let go of the idea that I could

always keep you safe. I had to endure the burden of supporting your decisions —however dumb."

We were quiet while she hung her head and scuffed her sneakers in the dirt. In that moment, she looked six years old, and it broke my heart. Wolfe was right; you can't go home again.

Aurora took in a long breath and sighed loudly, like the six-year-old she seemed to be. Then she slapped the bench and jumped forward. She landed in a superhero stance, one fist on the ground, the other held up behind her back.

"Nice," I said, *tsk*ing my disapproval.

"Watch this."

She shot up into the sky about a hundred feet, then roared back to the ground, stopping dead in the air two feet above it. She floated the last bit.

"You can fly?" I asked in awe.

"Nah, I can just go up and down like that once. Takes a few days off me, and now I'm going to need a nap."

"Superman will sleep a little easier."

Her face became suddenly serious.

"So I should train her and encourage her, even if it might get her killed? Assuming she still wants to be with me."

I shrugged.

"It worked for me," I said, "or at least it has so far. You should probably talk to Andrew and Augustine at least before you make any firm plans."

"Already did."

"And?"

"They said about the same thing, but without the gloating."

I raised an eyebrow.

"Okay, Augustine gloated too, but I told her I wouldn't tell you."

"My lips are sealed," I said, moving my fingers over my lips like closing a zipper.

"I mean it, Dad. You can't say anything."

I smiled knowingly, which made her growl.

Gloating indeed.

Thirteen

I guess Aurora took my advice, because the next day I saw them in the back yard of our residence practicing kata. I hadn't even known Miranda was in town, but it was none of my business anyway. I'm not the kind of father who sticks his nose in his daughter's love life. Nope. Not me.

I arrived in the back yard about ten minutes after Aurora had left for her shift to find Miranda still working on forms. She smiled when she saw me and smiled wider when she saw that I was carrying two soft-serve sundaes.

"You are the sweetest man," she said, reaching for one of the sundaes.

"Uh-uh. What makes you think one of these is for you? I could be very hungry."

Her smile never wavered. She put her hands on her hips and waited me out.

No sense letting a perfectly good sundae just melt.

We retired to the grass under a crimson maple tree that was empty of leaves. You didn't see these much in this part of the west.

"So," I said, crunching a maraschino cherry.

"So," she replied, capturing ice cream, hot fudge, and whipped cream expertly on the spoon and popping it in her mouth.

She was cagey, this one.

"How's life on the Left Hand of God?"

"That's it? No foreplay at all?

I choked a little, which made her laugh.

"You're blushing," she cackled.

"I am not, and don't change the subject."

Her eyebrows danced up and down.

Good Lord.

She patted my shoulder and wiped at the corner of her mouth.

"You are too easy to distract," she said.

"Again with the change of subject."

"The Left Hand of God is no doubt riddled with double agents and sellouts. It has lots of courageous people trying to make a difference, too. America is like Germany before the Second World War. We've got to fight back or we'll lose everything."

"You might lose yourself in the process."

She sucked on her spoon and narrowed her eyes.

"You know what's at stake. There are only ten of you and millions of them. I don't have time for ethical purity. Maybe my kids will live in a world where they can afford the niceties of non-violence. I want to give them that chance."

"You're willing to be the broken egg to make the omelet."

"If that's what it takes."

I looked into her eyes and realized that somewhere along the way she had become a soldier. Her face, her posture, all of it had changed, and I hadn't noticed before that moment.

"What happened while Aurora and I were away?"

She scraped the last of the hot fudge from the corners of the container and licked the spoon clean.

"I fucked up. I went back to my parents' house to get my computer. You said stay in hiding, and I did for about three months. I was cut off from everyone I knew. I figured after three months, nobody would be watching the house."

I cleared my throat.

"Like I said, I fucked up. *Anyway*, I zipped in through the cellar door, grabbed my computer and was headed out the same way when he jumped me. My parents have a little bar downstairs, and we went crashing over the table, broke a chair. He was trying to put something over my mouth, and I was flailing around when I grabbed a decanter.

My father has a couple of lead crystal decanters for his super special whiskeys. It has a long, thin neck and a big round bottom. When I swung it, the stopper came off and I flung whiskey in the guy's face. He just sputtered. He didn't loosen his grip. I don't know what I thought the whiskey would do, but he put the cloth over my face, and I just—"

She broke off for a moment to gather herself, her face stern with self-reproach.

"I just brained him. He went right down, and I kept hitting him until shit started oozing out of his ear. Then I threw up, and I was still shaking two hours after I got home. The computer was ruined, in case you wondered."

"That must have been awful."

"It was awful. The most awful part was that I felt so

powerless, like a child flailing against an adult, like I didn't have a chance. I couldn't live with that feeling, and I was tired of hiding. I sent Barbara an email. She has a regular email address like a normal person; I had no idea how to contact any of you when it happened."

"We were at sea, literally and figuratively. I'm sorry I wasn't there when you needed me."

Miranda nodded.

"Barbara joined the Left Hand. She's been working in Europe," she said.

"Barbara is supposed to be out of the game now. We left her in Morocco."

"Can't keep a good woman down. She inspired me. She didn't go softly into that good night. She's out there kicking ass and taking names. That's how I want to be, not helpless."

"And the guys on the boat?"

"I didn't have anything to lose. They made it clear that I was dead as soon as they got the word, and they didn't see me as any threat at all. They were so drunk that it wasn't hard."

"It wasn't technically hard to kill them, but what about the rest of it?"

"Look, Paul, I've done some stuff this year that I have to

push down, you know? I just lock it behind some door in my head because if I don't, I'm going to lose it, and I won't be able to fight. You know what that's like."

I do. It's not something you would wish on anyone.

"Those chickens will come home to roost one day," I said, looking into her face.

"And when they do, I'll deal with them, or I won't, or whatever. I can't think about that now."

Ants had found her empty ice cream container and were busily digging in the tiny crannies in the Styrofoam to get the last molecules of sugar. I watched them moving in a line from their hill and over the side of the container.

"What about Aurora?"

"I love her so much, but I'm not sure she still wants me, not the new me, anyway."

"I have it on good authority that you're wrong," I said rising, and not in any way shape or form meddling in my daughter's love life.

Fourteen

Night shift again. It was mid-January in a critical access hospital in Nebraska, only twenty beds. I had a seven-patient assignment. Five of them should have been in a nursing home, but these beds can be scarce in the best of times, and now those people with brain damage from the pandemic were taking places that used to be given to octogenarians.

All of my charges were asleep, thanks in part to a physician who had a heavy hand with sedating drugs. Some places don't allow this. They call it chemical restraint. Even if chemical restraints were illegal, we were still using them. The nursing shortage had gotten so bad that chemical restraints had become part of the solution. If the patients just sleep all the time, one nurse can take care of more of them.

So many nurses had died from the pandemic that some hospitals just shut down or became little more than hostels where people could die on a bed if they were lucky, on the floor if they weren't. Scores of nurses had been killed, or maimed, or just terrorized away from their jobs by the crush of protesters who accused them of being part of "the lie," a deep state conspiracy that hospitals had created the plague in order to harvest transplant organs for the rich.

One particularly vocal group opined that John F. Kennedy, Jr. would rise from the grave and help them take back the country. They huddled en masse, more than ten thousand by some estimates along Elm Street in Dallas. The leaders were fuzzy about why JFK, Jr. would be resurrected where his father had died, but who am I to judge? I'm a sorcerer who travels between dimensions.

Jr. was a no-show, but a swarm of Ether mosquitoes did show up, and it was a massacre, more than six thousand dead. The news was still playing ghastly footage of it when I got my lunch from the locker room fridge.

The room was dark, but the refrigerator light messed

with my night vision, because I heard him before I saw him. He was in the far corner of the room, quiet, his hands at his sides.

"Hello, Jude," I said, marshalling my will.

He took a step forward and held his hands out in front of him.

"That's close enough."

He stopped.

"Do you really think a few meters is going to make any difference if I came here to hurt you?" he asked, lighting a cigarette.

I waved my index finger and the flame went out. Then the cigarette split lengthwise, the tobacco fluttering to the ground.

He sighed.

"Let's do this outside," I said, dropping my lunch and loosening my shoulders. "No reason for the innocents to get hurt."

"Not this time, anyway," he responded and chuckled. "I'm not here to fight. I've come to warn you."

"Sure you have." I spread my feet and made a cage of my hands in front of me.

"Paul!" he said, his voice sharp. "You can't win. There's

too many of them now. They have too much power, and they are relentless hunters. Take the others somewhere away from here, an island or deep in the desert. It doesn't matter. Just go. If you stay here, they will kill you."

"I've been killed before. It wasn't the worst thing." That was as big a lie as I have ever told. A red ball of energy grew inside the cage of my hands.

"If I've found you, they will find you."

"You didn't bring them with you? You're slipping."

Jude laced his fingers behind his head and growled.

"Don't be an idiot," he hissed. "I'm trying to do the right thing."

"Uh-huh." The energy was the size of a soccer ball now.

"I have found a way to close the portal, to seal the worlds off from one another. I haven't told them. They would kill me for it; they want the gate to stay open. That's what gives them power. That's where the magic comes from, the opening between the two worlds."

"Keep talking," I said. "It's just about ready."

The energy launched from my hands to engulf Jude, but there was only empty space. I called it back to my hand like a yo-yo, and it seeped into my skin through the palm of my hand.

When I picked up my lunch, the tuna fish sandwich had burst out of its baggie and soaked everything else. I rinsed off the orange and made some peanut butter and graham cracker sandwiches from the patient supplies. Become a nurse and experience fabulous cuisine wherever you go; they always have peanut butter and crackers.

I ate at the nurses' station while watching cat videos on my phone. Sometimes I just couldn't do more than that. In making my rounds, I found Eloise sitting up on the side of her bed. The shade was pulled up, and she was looking out past the lights of the parking lot to the stars and the prairie. I knelt down beside her.

"Can I get you anything, Ms. Landry?"

She was younger than my current incarnation, but she patted my head as if she was a spinster and I a little boy.

"We're all gonna die," she said, slurring the words. She had regained some speech, but I had to listen carefully to understand her.

"We're all going to die," I agreed. "Sooner or later."

She frowned and flapped her right hand at the wrist, then shook her head.

"We're all gonna die," she repeated, louder, more emphatic this time.

"That is the long and short of it," I said and began to rise. She put a trembling hand on my shoulder and pushed me back down. She looked right into my eyes. The skin under her left eye twitched as she brought her brows together.

"S-s-soon," she said, like a sigh. She looked at me even harder, making sure I got the full meaning.

It was spooky as shit.

Fifteen

Knowing we were vulnerable after Jude's appearance, we scattered and, for the moment, abandoned all hope of doing any nursing work. None of us knew the others' locations. We agreed to meet up on the secure dark web meeting room James had set up for us when the internet was little more than online bulletin boards.

Without his help, we had some trouble getting through all the security. Bart and Phil were able to clear most of it up, although the voice and picture was wonky.

Peter, Bart, and Phil were in one box. They were on the boat somewhere in the Atlantic Ocean. The rest of us joined from our hideouts. Mine was in Maine. I broke into a vacation home I had rented on Mt. Dessert Island years before. The owners only used it for a few weeks in the summer, and I had lived there during a winter and spring contract. They were too rich to worry about buttoning the house up for winter, so the heat and electric were still on. They'd be suspicious when they got the bill, if they even paid their own bills. They were the kind of rich who had people for things like bill-paying.

My colleagues looked like hell, Andrew being the worst. His beard was unkempt, and he had deep purple half-moons under his eyes. Simon, of course, looked great in the way he looked bad. He could even make exhausted look sexy. The boat people --Peter, Bart, and Phil-- were tanned, but all looked to have lost weight. Aurora was a fidgeting mess.

Augustine organized something on the desk in front of her before calling the council to order.

"The Left Hand has relayed some intel about James. He's being held in the presidential bunker in Cheyenne Mountain. According to reports, he's under constant guard by one man, a presidential envoy. Our best guess at this point is Thagirion. That can't be a coincidence."

Thagirion is James's opposite among the Returned. He

must have been using suppressive magic, or they were keeping James sedated, or both.

Thomas turned his head and muttered a curse. "So let's go," he said, slapping the table in front of him. "We can have him out of there by this time tomorrow."

"They have two brigades of soldiers and three squadrons of aircraft protecting that bunker," Augustine said, talking over Thomas. She must have turned his mic off, because he was gesticulating wildly, but we couldn't hear anything.

"What about moving through rock, like they did in the Arctic?" Andrew asked. He didn't look up when he said it, so he knew it probably wasn't a viable option.

"The rock is reinforced. There are booby-traps above and below, and you can bet it will be warded. A frontal assault is not an option."

"What is their plan for him? Do we know what they will do? They can't hold him forever," Peter complained. "Perhaps they will be vulnerable when they move him."

We all looked at Augustine, which was disorienting in a virtual meeting. Each member of the council was looking in a different direction, but I knew we were all looking at her, waiting for her orders.

"Miranda?" Augustine said.

She appeared in Aurora's screen.

"She is not a member of the council. This is highly irregular," Peter protested, but Augustine shushed him with a gesture.

"I'll be brief. I know I'm not supposed to be here," Miranda began. "We have a mole on the president's staff. She's not a player. She's one of those invisible administrative people. She said they're setting up a courtroom in the East Wing. There's going to be a show trial. She didn't know who it was for, but she said the president was insisting it be carried world-wide. He was bitching about the lack of interest by the foreign press."

"When?" I asked, clenching my jaw.

"President's Day."

"That's less than a month away," Andrew murmured.

Thomas jumped up and was pointing at the screen, but we still couldn't hear him.

"Jude told Paul the Returned are everywhere looking for us. We have to assume that Cheyenne Mountain is a trap. They will want to draw us out, at least to do reconnaissance," said Augustine.

At this, Thomas grew still and slumped into his chair. He raised his hand, and Augustine nodded.

"We can't just leave him there," Thomas said, on the verge of tears.

"We're not leaving him," Augustine replied. "We're going to take it to those fuckers, but not on their terms."

"What if they just kill him?" asked Andrew. "Just send him back for a rebirth. That knocks us down ten percent. By the time he's ready for an awakening, the Returned will control the whole planet."

"Not necessarily," Thomas said.

"No," I spat, cutting him off. "We agreed a long time ago. It's not safe and it's not ethical."

"We felt that way about possessing a vessel, too," he replied pointing to himself.

"Thomas, I have explained this in how many different lives?" said Andrew. "And we know more now about how the brain develops. Awakening an infant might seriously damage its brain, and constant magic --there's no telling how it would affect development."

We get older with each use of magic. It's why we can't just cure all of our patients; we wouldn't last a year. We have to save magic, dole it out slowly. Even so, most of us have old bodies by the time we're in our forties. In the sixteen hundreds, during the Black Death, Thomas had a theory that if we could find a newborn knight just after reincarnation and awaken them, they would be fully conscious and could use magic to grow in a space of days. Three or four big spells and they'd be adolescents. The problem is that a baby's brain isn't set up to absorb and process nine hundred years of living. We had never tried it, and I doubted we would try it now.

"We don't need to resolve that tonight," Augustine admonished. "But we do need to plan an offensive, and we need to coordinate it with the Left Hand."

"That's suicide," cried Thomas. "They sold us out less than two months ago."

"Surely," Augustine said, smiling, "a council of sorcerers can figure a way to vet our partners."

I did not like the sound of that, and judging by the look on her face, neither did Miranda.

Sixteen

The last weekend in January found Andrew and me in New Orleans. We needed to know that we could trust the local chapter of the Left Hand of God to keep up their end of our plan to rescue James. The Big Easy had done pretty well during the pandemic. They were accustomed to dealing with mosquitoes, and while the ones from the Ether that killed millions weren't exactly the same, the local denizens knew how to keep unwanted bugs away.

New Orleans was one of several cities where mayhem would stretch the federal government's resources thin. Augustine had mobilized Left Hand groups all over the country, from Seattle to Miami. The idea was to cascade the riots over several hours in the two days leading up to President's Day and James's trial. New Orleans was set to explode at midnight on Sunday.

The civil unrest would start with a pile-up in the Mississippi River. The Left Hand was going to set a couple of fishing boats on fire and let them sink near shore on each side of the river. That would bring out the Coast Guard and local cops and create an opportunity to raise some hell.

The plan depended on one guy, a chain-smoking communist who went by Noah.

"Just Noah," he said, crushing a butt between a calloused forefinger and thumb. "Like the ark guy."

"We know who Noah is, thanks," chirped Andrew. He was swinging between periods of silence and motionlessness to hyperactivity. I didn't need to be a shrink to know what that meant.

"What do you wanna know?" Noah asked.

Noah was tall and lanky with the kind of flat muscles that come from manual labor. He had a PhD in political philosophy from Brown, so it didn't make sense that he spent his time unloading trucks at a grocery wholesale.

"So, Dr. Noah. Why are you on the loading dock?"

"Nothing to lose but my chains," he said through pursed lips while lighting another coffin nail. "The warehouse sends trucks all over the South. It makes a good central distribution hub."

"Distributing what, exactly?" asked Andrew, leaning in and obliterating Noah's personal space. Noah didn't flinch. He just shrugged and flicked a cigarette ash away from Andrew.

"This and that. Listen, the guys at Pagoda said you were legit, but I don't know you or what you really want. Everybody has an angle, and I can't see yours yet. So before you give me the third degree, I've got some questions."

Andrew spun on the man, but I got between them.

"Be cool," I whispered. "Just relax"

Turning to Noah, I said, "We're an ancient group of, well, sorcerers. One of our brothers was taken by Roosevelt's crew, and we need to get him back before the president and his people do terrible things to him."

"Lotta people been disappeared since the election. Why should I risk my people for you? Call me a skeptic about the magic thing, but your story sounds like one more opiate for the masses."

Andrew opened his hands and the ground swallowed

Noah up to his neck. He tried to move his arms, and failing, nodded appreciatively, the cigarette still dangling from his mouth. I raised my hands by my side, and Noah rose to stand next to us. He flicked the ash from his cigarette before crushing it out and throwing it into the trashcan on the corner.

"Okay, so you're sorcerers. Impressive," he said. "Why do you need us?"

"Because," I said, "Roosevelt is a sorcerer too. Some of his key people as well. The guy running Homeland Security is a particular baddie. We can't beat them without help."

Noah looked at the ground, nodding.

"The city has gone to shit. Don't get me wrong, it was plenty shitty before Roosevelt, but it was a place I knew, a place I understood. Now," He gestured toward the street behind us. "Now we've got National Guard breaking up second lines and rounding up anybody doing hoodoo, even if it's just a show for the saps from out of town. I don't recognize this place anymore."

"Then you'll help us?"

Andrew stopped pacing when I asked. He was using magic. I could feel it, like tendrils reaching out to Noah, slipping under his skin and into his ears.

"It's not up to just me. I'm not a king." He smiled then, and I could see that one of his teeth was broken. "I'll recommend it to my comrades. Come to Pagoda in two days. Order the breakfast burrito, extra hot."

He scanned the street around us and jogged to an alley between two shotgun-style houses and was gone.

I turned to Andrew and raised an eyebrow. He was pale in the glow of the streetlight. Some neighborhoods in New Orleans had the ability to swallow the light from the rest of the city. Under each streetlight lived a little shaft of brightness that did nothing to obscure the thick blanket of night and the spray of stars above. I don't know any other city in the world that could do that.

"He's who he says he is," Andrew said at last. "He's got demons, no doubt about it, and he's angry. He's lost someone close recently. I wandered around his mind long enough to know that he's telling the truth. He reminded me of you a little."

"Me? You've gone for a stroll in my head?"

A sad smile spread across his face.

"We've been friends for too long for you to have any secrets."

"Still. Privacy?"

"Yeah," he said. "Sorry. I've got a hankering for coffee and beignets."

"A hankering? What are you, a thousand years old?"

"You're stealing quips from Aurora? That is just sad."

"*You're* just sad," I said in my best witty-rejoinder voice. That showed him.

Seventeen

Andrew and I slunk back to the coffins set atop our native soil for five hours of sleep broken by, in my case, angry dreams of battle and blood spilled. I didn't bother Andrew about my anxiety or the certainty that we were moving toward another defining conflict for the order. Andrew was in no shape to deal with my dreams anyway.

He was crying softly when I woke up, rocking a little back and forth. I massaged his shoulders and kissed the top of his head before sitting cross-legged facing him. His face was a mask of pain, and it was hard to look at. We touched foreheads, arms on each other's shoulders while I waited for him to gain some composure.

"I can't go on like this forever," he said at last, drawing back and wiping his nose. "James can't handle this. He's, he's not really a warrior anymore."

I nodded.

"It's got to stop," he said, his voice ringing with finality. "No more. I don't care if I have to stay in the Ether. This is it. I'm not coming back."

"Jude says he knows how to close the gate. You might get your chance. If we can't move between worlds, you should get stuck there when you die here."

"Jude," Andrew hissed. It was so unlike him to have venom in his voice. He was the calm center of our whole order, and he was coming completely unraveled. I hadn't seen him like this since the Black Death. That was when his interest in psychology (we called it philosophy back then) replaced his faith.

"I know, but I can't work out any motive for giving me that warning. Homeland Security broke into our apartment in Salt Lake two days after we left. Either it was all an elaborate act, or he really didn't tell them until after we were gone."

He muttered and picked at the grass beside him, and I

had no idea how to handle him.

"Time for breakfast," I said, jumping up. "I'm *hankering* for a breakfast burrito."

"Asshole," he muttered.

A line of people snaked around the deck at Pagoda. The place had the tiled roof from which it drew its name, open windows for ordering, like an ice cream shop, and picnic tables under a roof beside it. We got our food and sat in the shade of the table closest to the building.

"They're doing a brisk business," I said, which made Andrew snort.

"Next time you decide to make small talk to break the tension, just use semaphore. It will be more subtle."

I bit into my burrito so that I wouldn't scathe Andrew with a retort. I don't know what I was going to say, but it would have been epic. I bit into a hard piece of plastic, pushing it into my cheek and staring at Andrew. He got the hint.

There was a little triangle of dried up grass and a few scrawny trees across the road from Pagoda that the city has designated a park. It's about four steps side-to-side at its widest, so someone at city hall was having a laugh. Nonetheless, we ducked behind one of said scrawny trees, and I took the plastic out of my mouth.

It looked like a thick coffee stirrer. Someone had etched the word "DONE" onto its face.

"That Noah is a man of few words," Andrew chided.

"At least for us."

We were interrupted by sirens as four patrol cars skidded to a stop in front of and alongside Pagoda. Tires squealed behind the building where they stored their supplies and had their kitchen. Police flew out of their cars, guns drawn, and swarmed into the restaurant. There were screams, and then a man and a woman stumbled through the door. The man was white with dirty blond dreads that were drenched in blood. The woman was brown and doubled over, grasping at her stomach.

Andrew turned and walked toward the scene. I grabbed his shoulder, and he flung me ten meters into a wooden fence.

"I am a knight of the Order of St. John of Jerusalem." His voice boomed and echoed. "Leave this place and never return." In each hand a flaming blade appeared, the length of a good hunting knife.

His declaration was met with gunfire, the bullets melting into mist before they could reach him. One of the officers was saying something into a radio before Andrew threw the knife in his left hand and the blade buried itself into the officer's head.

Andrew's weapons were not the crude killing things that the rest of us used. He was our consigliere, our confessor; his power lay in the minds and hearts of the people he touched. When the blade was no longer visible, the knife's handle evaporated. The officer stood up straight, a look of utter panic on his face.

"Withdraw!" he yelled. "Retreat! Get the fuck out of here." The officers around him looked at him and then at Andrew, who was balancing his remaining knife in his right hand and scanning the men and women in blue, picking his next target.

The first officer's panic spread as if a switch had been thrown, and they sprinted to their cars, disappearing in clouds of burning rubber and squealing tires. I limped toward Andrew, who held his hand out and stopped me cold.

"Don't do this," I said, loud enough for him to hear me. "This isn't going to help James."

Andrew crossed the parking lot to the young people on the ground. He touched the white man's head, and the blood was gone. The injury must have been fatal before Andrew's touch, because I saw his back stoop and his shoulders hunch.

The woman was sitting on the ground in a pool of blood, keening. She stilled as soon as Andrew touched her. His hair turned white, and I realized the woman must have been pregnant, the blood, a miscarriage.

"Andrew, no, stop!" I wailed and banged my fists against the invisible wall he had erected to keep me out.

The skin on his arms sagged and was covered in dark spots. His lips moved, rustling the paper-thin skin of his face. The woman gasped and put her hand to her abdomen, her eyes filling with tears, and the avatar of Andrew the Apostle turned to ash that blew away with the breeze.

Eighteen

I fell, pole-axed to the street. I couldn't take my eyes off the place where Andrew had been, where the young couple now held each other and sobbed. Andrew had saved them all, perhaps bringing the baby back to life, and it took all of him.

He hadn't cared.

I don't know how long I knelt in the street, which was quiet now that the sirens had stopped. I swayed, I'm sure of that, before strong hands slid under my armpits and hauled me to my feet.

"Time to go," a deep voice said, and Noah was half-pushing, half-dragging me into a courtyard, before shutting and locking the gate behind us.

People filtered into the yard in ones and twos. Black, brown, and white people, men and women, young and old. They murmured and kept their distance from us, but they were more curious than angry.

"This is one of them," Noah said, lifting his head to address the crowd, and there was more murmuring.

"His friend saved Lorna and Dominick."

"Chased the cops away."

"Where did he go?"

"Yeah, where is he?"

Noah quieted them and looked to me.

"He's gone," I said, my voice thick. "He used his life to save your friends," I swallowed hard, "and their baby."

The chattering became louder and more agitated. Noah waved his arms to quiet them.

"We've got to get him out of here," he said at last. A big man of indeterminate age waved toward Noah. He was standing behind an old blue pickup truck with crab traps and rope in the back. The man's beard and mustache were so thick I couldn't see his mouth.

"I can take him as far as Biloxi," the man said.

Noah nodded and moved me toward the truck. I don't remember most of the next few minutes. There was a hidden compartment under the bed of the truck. It was cramped and smelled of fish and gasoline, but I got inside without protest, and when I was next aware, the bearded man was opening the compartment and introducing me to a Black woman standing beside a white panel truck. There was a bed inside, and I slept.

We spoke not a word during my time in the van. When I woke up, we were at a rest stop in the shade of tall hemlock trees. She was sitting at a picnic table, food and a thermos in front of her.

I reached out my hand and said, "I'm Paul."

She looked at my hand and didn't take it.

"No names," was all she said.

We ate in silence. The coffee was hot and bitter. The sunlight beyond the trees was bright. All of the nuance had gone out of the world. Half an hour after I finished eating, a sports car eased into the rest area. The woman with me tensed, but the tension left her when the car flashed its lights.

An Asian man in khakis and a lime green polo shirt stepped out of his car, doffed an imaginary hat at the woman, and gestured towards the car. I looked between the two of them.

"He's alright," she said and surprised me with an embrace before disappearing into the van.

I slid into a leather seat next to the Asian man, who stared at me while I fastened my seat belt.

"You can call me Chet," he said, starting the car. "I know who you are."

We drove for most of the day, finally stopping at a campground just outside of Hickory, North Carolina, beside a long, narrow lake. He pulled up to an Airstream that looked as though the forest was eating it. There was a soft light in the window behind the shade, probably a lantern.

"This is as far as I go," Chet said. They were the only words he had spoken to me in more than seven hours. He had fed me, road food mostly, crappy sandwiches, chips, and soda, but we hadn't talked. As soon as I shut the car door, he slipped onto the campground's dirt road and his taillights disappeared into the night.

I should have taken precautions before entering the trailer. I had no idea who would be inside, but I was still numb, so I just knocked on the door. It opened, and there was Augustine. When she saw me, her hand flew to her mouth and she pulled me to her. I felt Simon and Thomas wrap around us, too.

We stood in the lantern light, just inside the door. My shirt was wet. Augustine's shirt was wet. I was deaf for the moment, hollowed out.

Thomas broke the hug first, leading me inside. At the tiny kitchen table a pile of dark electronics anchored four corners of a hand-drawn map. Simon handed me a bottle of some kind of alcohol. I took a long pull before sitting down and looking dumbly at the map.

"Andrew was reborn this morning," I said at last. My cheeks were warm slashes, and drops fell from them onto the map.

"What happened?" Augustine asked, her voice low, like you would talk to a wild animal.

I told them. When I got to the part about the pregnancy, Simon gasped and Thomas swore, but Augustine just looked grim.

"The others are on their way," she said. "The campground is owned by a member of the Left Hand. It's off-season, so we don't have to worry about anybody out here."

I nodded and Thomas squeezed my shoulder.

"We really needed him," mumbled Simon, which drew a sharp look from Thomas.

When I raised my head, my friends were all looking at me with pity or compassion; sometimes it's hard to tell the difference.

"You should have seen him," I said, my smile stretching my tear-streaked face. "He was magnificent."

Nineteen

Thomas and I walked by the lake at dusk, lost in our thoughts. An owl called far off in the forest and was answered by another close to us. Thomas cocked his head the tiniest bit, listening, but never broke stride.

"We good?" I asked.

"Just an owl," he replied turning toward the lake to watch fish make ripples in the still water, rising for bugs.

"It feels like we've already lost."

"It ain't over until the bariatric woman with the beautiful voice finishes her song," I said.

"Well ain't you woke as fuck."

"What can we do but fight on? We've lost before. We've been wiped out before."

"Feels different this time," Thomas said, stopping to skip a flat rock out into the lake. I counted twenty-five jumps.

"Did you put a little extra on that?"

"Just me, no mojo."

"Damn."

The radio was on low when we got back to the trailer, with NPR reporting that more than sixty million Americans had now died from the pandemic. The casualty figures made Thomas wince, not just for the loss of life, but because he felt some responsibility for all the deaths. The fruit of his tree had borne the deadly mosquitoes into our world. There was no way he could have known that would happen, but he still blamed himself.

Aurora did the same. The rift through which the bugs had dropped had been opened for her. She hadn't known, none of us had known, that the ripe dates that came spilling from the Ether were full of insects. There was no way we could have predicted how ordinary people would react to getting bitten, either. Having been practicing Catholics for centuries, we were experts at self-flagellation.

Aurora's mood had improved some since Miranda joined us. Aurora's partner now had a dueling scar across her jawline on the left from a cut from a broken bottle in a street fight in Portland, Oregon. Aurora wanted to magic it away, but Miranda wouldn't hear of it. She said she came by it honest and wanted to keep it as a souvenir.

The radio began broadcasting from the White House press room. Ghagiel, I don't remember the name of the vessel he was using, read a statement warning the public about the rise of terror everywhere in our country. Communism, the red menace, was sweeping the nation, according to the statement.

"These seditious monks want to destroy our way of life, to pervert it beyond all recognition. They must be found, and they must be exterminated. We cannot fail. We will not fail. Our country will be a Christian nation once again. We will let the Bible and our Lord and Savior be our guides, and we will banish the wicked forever."

Simon clicked the radio off.

"At least he didn't come right out and say that Thaumiel is our lord and savior."

"Small mercies," Augustine huffed.

"You're getting to him," Miranda said, refilling her

coffee cup. She drank coffee at all hours of the day and night, just like, well, just like a nurse. "You made it to a prime time address."

"Well done, us," Thomas chimed in.

"In a few days, it won't matter," said Augustine. "In a few days, this will be over, one way or another."

"About that," I began. "Why shouldn't Aurora and I be in the building as well? If the plan is to assault the White House with all of us, shouldn't we all be inside?"

Augustine took a deep breath.

"We've been over this several times. I'm giving you the benefit of the doubt and assuming you're not just whining, so I'll go over it again. The rest of us will be stone."

"Including Bart and Phil," Simon interrupted.

"The rest of us will be stone," Augustine said, beginning again. "You know how tricky that can be, even for a few minutes. For two days it will be disorienting. We need to be sure someone remains in human form to wake us up in case we start believing we are sandstone pillars. You are the seneschal of the Order. When you call us, we will come. Aurora is a powerful sorcerer, but she has never assumed such an alien form for so long. We don't want to lose her before the party even starts. What part of that don't you understand?"

I looked at my feet.

"I was just whining."

"I thought so."

"How sure are we about the journalists? Thomas asked. "If anything goes wrong with the press swap, we're done."

"I checked them out personally," Miranda answered, "all six."

"We'll only have one chance. It's the only press conference before the trial."

"I get it," Miranda replied, staring at him. "I know what's at stake. I'm with the backup group if it goes sideways, but I know it's long odds if we get to that point."

"Okay, okay," Thomas said. "We've been in the shit like this before, and it did not go well."

"Saved some lives," I pointed out.

"But we all died," Thomas retorted.

"We died for a while."

Miranda looked at us quizzically.

"Historically, we have bad luck around pandemics," I explained. "Everyone died in the Bubonic plague."

"Some of us more than once," Simon added.

"We all remember," I agreed. "It was a long plague, and

you had particularly bad luck."

"Luck," Simon grumbled.

"Thomas is talking about the Spanish Flu," Augustine explained. "During the First World War."

"That was a doozy," I said. "But it's not really my story to tell."

"Jamie's not here to tell it," Thomas replied.

"Alright then."

I cleared my throat.

"It was 1915, and we were all attached to the British Royal Fusileers . . ."

Twenty

No one moved as I took a sip of beer and cleared my throat. What was left of the council was spread over chairs and benches and one of the beds. Augustine nodded at me encouragingly.

"Augustine and I had one tour in Belgium early in the war before we joined the others in the eighty-sixth brigade. We cared for men in the trenches. They said women didn't fight back then, but one of our best friends, Edith Cavell, a nurse, worked in the trenches with us. She took care of German soldiers too, but they killed her for helping some of the Brits escape.

"On Gallipoli, it was the Ottomans again. They fucking routed us. Push after push, they turned us back. We were in those bloody fucking trenches for months. It was like living in a cesspool, human shit everywhere. And body parts sometimes stuck in among the sandbags. When you thought you'd eat a bullet before you would take one more day, some idiot officer would blow a whistle and we'd go over the top."

Miranda looked up, her face a question.

"You'd climb over the top of the trench and start running into the enemy's machine gun fire," Simon murmured.

"Over the top, boys!" Thomas barked.

"Sometimes we crawled on our bellies," Augustine explained. "There might be the tiniest cover made by craters in the dirt from artillery shells."

"Sometimes you had to crawl on your belly under barbed wire," Thomas said.

"If you got wounded there, it was tough to get you out," I added.

"I didn't think that was the worst part," Augustine said. "I had to go over behind the men and try to rescue the wounded. We charged during breaks between artillery barrages. They'd be shelling you, sometimes for an hour without stop, endless, ground shuddering, ear-bursting blasts, one after the other. As soon as our charge stalled or we fell back, the shelling would start again. I got caught out many times."

We were quiet then. Miranda and Aurora scanned the room, but we were all lost in memories of those terrible days.

"Andrew had a trench gun," Augustine said, and Thomas winced. "It was a shotgun with a bayonet attached. It was used for blasting the enemy when we got into their trenches. Used at very close range."

"Andrew did that?" Aurora whispered.

No one said anything.

"James was Perpetua in that life," I continued. "She was in the nurse corps, like Augustine. She did her best, and she saved many lives, but she, like James, was not made for combat anymore. By the end of 1915, she couldn't go over anymore. She couldn't eat, couldn't do much of anything.

"Our commander got a call from headquarters to quarantine anyone with certain symptoms, with influenza. They were worried about it spreading through the troops in the trenches. Perpetua has some foresight, and she had a vision of millions of dead, shrouds piled taller than a house.

She said this flu was another plague."

"Wait," Aurora interrupted. "The first Spanish flu cases didn't come until 1918."

"Spoiler alert," quipped Simon, but there was no mirth in his voice.

The others nodded solemnly.

"Then we got hell on earth, an artillery barrage that we thought would never end. My teeth were chipped from the concussions. We were too disoriented to do anything when it stopped. I was deaf for a while; I couldn't hear anything but a ringing. We didn't get the machine guns up quick enough. They were on us. We fought with bayonets and pistols. Andrew laid about him with the trench gun. We were too exhausted and rattled to draw on any magic.

"I don't know how long it went on like that, hand-to-hand. Jude was with me; I'd almost forgotten that. He and I fought back-to-back like we had in Malta, and like Malta all of our efforts just slowed the enemy down. We couldn't turn the tide. Eventually we were all hemmed in, and it was just us, just the knights. Perpetua was in the middle. We protected her from the worst of it.

"I knew we were done for," I said, stopping for a moment.

"We all knew," Augustine said.

"It was a feeling of such powerlessness, such hopelessness. We knew we would die, and there was nothing we could do. We fought desperately over the bodies of our fallen comrades, but it was futile.

"Then Perpetua said, 'The flu. We can do something about that at least.' I didn't think I'd heard her the first time, but she wanted us all to join hands, to do a spell together, to do something worthwhile in our last moments. This was the first time, before we banished Jude. So we did. We dropped our weapons and joined together, and a light flowed out of us as we were gunned down in the trench. I saw it shoot into the sky before I was lying on my back in the Wastes, you know, in the Ether."

"But you didn't stop the flu," Aurora said. "It infected a third of the world."

"All that magic bought humanity two years, that's all. That's how powerful a disease like that can be."

"Christ," Miranda murmured.

"He had nothing to do with it."

Twenty-One

The Friday before Labor Day, and we had assembled one last time at the counter of a diner in Chester, Vermont. A large television faced us from the corner of the room. The sound was muted, but the waitress turned it up when Augustine asked. There was no one else in the place anyway, and we all had glamor going so that no one would call the National Guard. This was on Friday. James's trial was Monday evening, so as to get the prime time crowd.

"He wasn't scheduled to have a press conference today," Thomas observed.

That made us all wary. We were counting on tomorrow's

press conference to get into the White House. Roosevelt didn't usually talk to the public two days in a row. Augustine shushed us.

Ghagiel introduced the president, and there he was, Thaumiel himself. He smiled and waved, although the room looked empty. The network played an applause track, a little too late, which exposed the artifice.

"That was our guys," Miranda said proudly. Aurora had given her a beard and heavy eyebrows with her glamor, and her high, light voice was utterly incongruous. "Our guys slowed the soundtrack so everyone would know it was bullshit."

The president made a quieting motion with his hands, and again, there was a little delay before the applause petered out. Miranda snickered as Thaumiel adjusted the microphone. He was in the rose garden, an area typically used for signing important legislation. Behind him, just out of focus, was what appeared to be a wide tree stump with a "U" worn out of it's center.

"Good afternoon," said the president, smiling and looking from side to side to continue the illusion that people were sitting before him. "Justice triumphs." He paused to let that sink in.

"You people, you proud Christians, you who have been with me from the start, you have brought about this moment. It is your victory, your triumph, your justice. Our Homeland Security is the greatest law enforcement agency in history. They have captured or killed thousands of traitors, people who would lead this country into the arms of the communists and the anarchists, the homos and weirdos and the Black nationalists and the Hebrew terrorists. They are making America clean again for all you good folks.

"When I said, 'don't be too gentle with the prisoners,' you cheered me, because you know justice. When I said, 'not everyone *deserves* due process,' you marched in the streets to say yes to real justice. And your supreme court upheld that justice." (more belated applause)

"But what about the Red Monks, the scourge of those communist zealots who have plagued us from the very beginning? They kidnap children and keep them in cages with only a litter box for a toilet, and they feed these children a steady diet of lies. That's right: lies for breakfast, lunch, and dinner. They tell the little children" (here he adopts a sing-song voice) "'there's no God, your parents are monsters, you can be a kitty cat if you want to be, a boy cat or a girl cat, and you don't have to obey anyone.'

"That's the filth they rain down on these poor children. How can they resist? We have saved many thousands, tens of thousands even." (Applause track, which he lets go on until it is obviously repeating itself) "How can these tortured children have justice?"

The background behind the president came into focus slowly. Thomas was the first to realize what it was.

"No," he scoffed. "It's just a stunt. They wouldn't really use that. They're bluffing."

"It's a chopping block," Augustine said, her voice low.

A woman was dragged into the scene by two men in black. The men wore riot helmets; the woman had a black hood over her head. She stumbled, and they hauled her steadily across the lawn. Augustine's head tilted as she watched the screen.

"Oh, no," Miranda whispered.

"More coffee?" asked our waiter, glimpsing the screen from the corner of her eye. "What's he up to now?" she asked.

"A beheading," I answered.

"He's so dramatic, but I gotta say he's done great things for the schools. Since they reinstituted corporal punishment, my kids are all 'yes sir' and 'no ma'am.' My parents hit me, and I turned out all right. It had gotten way too permissive, if you ask me. Discipline never hurt anybody."

She complained about the changes in her town, which I took as code for 'some black people have moved here.' She wore a black polo shirt with a name tag. Her bangs were teased up, eighties style. I guess the hair helped to draw the gaze away from her lumpy sparkle eye shadow.

Her voice became background noise when they pulled the hood off the woman, now standing behind the block. Augustine gasped.

"It's impossible. She's not even in the country," she said.

"She's part of the Left Hand," Miranda murmured. "She couldn't stay away."

Augustine made a choked sound, which elicited something dismissive from the waitress that I didn't hear. On national TV, our seer, Barbara, stood behind the chopping block, her head shaved, her face defiant. Augustine toppled backward, knocking plates and cups to the ground.

"Calm down, lady, geez," the waitress whined, and snapped her gum. "Why don't –"

She was cut off by a loud slap that rocked her backward. Miranda loomed over the counter.

"Shut. The fuck. Up. Unless you want some more."

The waitress rubbed at her now reddening cheek, spun, and rushed through the double doors leading to the kitchen.

On the screen, the two men pushed Barbara down, her neck fitting into the depression in the middle of the block. She was yelling something, but the broadcast had muted it.

"My friends, this is justice. This is the only kind of deterrent these animals understand. This is one of the Red Monks, red for the blood they spill, red for their tyrannical communism. Today we cut off one of the snake's heads," said Roosevelt in his calm and reasonable baritone.

He lifted Barbara's head by her chin so that her face looked at the camera. Her mouth made the words clearly, but none of her words were broadcast. "Die, you motherfuckers."

The president extended his hand, and a flaming sword appeared. Simon, our fire mage, ground his fist so hard into the countertop that it charred. The president lifted the sword with two hands and yelled, "For justice!" before separating Barbara's head from her body. The head rolled on the grass, and the camera closed in on it, her eyelids twitching furiously. There was no blood. The sword had cauterized the wound as it cut through flesh.

"That was the first time we've seen the flaming sword

actually used, Robert," said one newscaster.

"He's sending a message to his political opponents," replied the other. "I think the use of fire is particularly significant."

"And the lack of blood."

"Absolutely. 'Making a clean break with the past,' perhaps?"

Augustine's eyes were ablaze, and there were sirens in the distance.

"Time to go," Thomas said, putting some bills on the counter. "We've got a long drive ahead of us."

Twenty-Two

At Greenfield, Massachusetts, we disbursed into five different cars, all taking different routes to Washington. I was assigned to drive west to Binghamton, New York, then south on Interstate 81. This road was full of truckers late at night, roaring by. I kept the car to five miles per hour over the limit, which left me forever in the right lane.

I didn't have to be in Washington until tomorrow afternoon, so I could afford to get a hot meal at a truck stop and fill my thermos with coffee. While I understood my role in the plan, I wasn't happy about it.

Reporters wouldn't come to press conferences unless

they were in full insect-proof suits. The White House could not allow the press corps to be seen taking these precautions, because it ran counter to the narrative that the pandemic was a hoax.

On the other hand, the president couldn't shut out the press altogether, particularly since he had bribed, blackmailed, or threatened many of the networks into favorable coverage. The compromise was green suits. By wearing green protective suits, the White House communications office could use a green screen to run videos of the press corps in prior briefings —conferences during the last administration— and overlay the live feed.

It was clunky and awkward, and the reporters' mouths were obviously out of sync with their voices, but at least there was a semblance of real coverage. Reporters donned and doffed the green suits in a special room in the basement before lumbering up for a briefing.

This would be our only chance. The knights --Augustine, Simon, Thomas, Peter, Philip, and Bartholomew-- would take the place of six sympathetic journalists and attend the conference. You heard right; Barbara's beheading had brought even Peter, the head of our order, into the fight. We were all in to rescue James.

When the conference was over, they would return to the basement room to take off their suits, but instead of leaving, they would flow into the rock and up into the pillars of the portico facing the south lawn. They would have to remain in the stone for almost two full days. This is why we couldn't chance Aurora in the assault team; she had never had to hold a transformation that long.

Also, getting them out of the city was going to be a bitch. Miranda said she would have members of the Left Hand in the crowd with us, but I was not reassured. There could be a hundred thousand people around the south lawn; that was too big a tide to control, no matter how much magic you had.

Roosevelt would preside over the "trial" from the Truman Balcony on the second floor. When I gave the signal, the six of them would materialize on the lawn, free James, and run like hell.

The Left Hand was going to set off an explosion at the Renwick Gallery near Lafayette Square when James's trial began. Aurora, Miranda, and I would be in the crowd of rubberneckers on E Street. We had a getaway van parked in the underground lot at the OAS. Our job was to get the knights through the mayhem by whatever means necessary.

I had the secondary job of awakening anyone stuck in their pillar. It was possible through two days of waiting to forget that you were a living, breathing being, and to become the stone. It seemed unlikely, but we had to be prepared. If necessary, I was to loose a lightning strike. That would give them a big entrance.

As I drove in the dark on I-81, I should have been relaxing. So many big battles, so many impossible odds in the centuries of my being that it should have felt like just another Tuesday. It did not.

The Returned had turned the tide, flung open the gate between our worlds. We surmised that the only reason we hadn't been overrun was that our allies in the Ether were stemming the flow, making the Returned fight there as well as here, keeping a wave of cogs from bursting through.

Our plan to thin out federal resources was having mixed results. The protests and riots had begun in Las Vegas, Eugene, Olympia, and San Jose. Federal troops had been dispatched from California, and the local National Guards, along with the current equivalent of brown shirts and black shirts, was doing battle with the resistance on city streets.

Three protesters had been killed by rubber bullets in Olympia, twenty had met a similar fate in Vegas, but this time with lead. The protests rolled east towards Washington as I made my way south.

My daughter would be in this battle. She had gone on missions before, but never to war. This was an all-or-nothing play, and there was a very real chance some or all of us would die. We didn't know if Aurora would be reborn. This could kill her for real, her young life snuffed out forever.

To be honest, Andrew's death still haunted me. He had been unraveled at the end, unable to endure one more minute of outrage. He had given his life to save three people. It seemed a poor bargain to me. I hoped Andrew had been satisfied. It would be a couple of decades at least before I could know.

I picked up I-70 in Hagerstown, Maryland, and stopped for a bite to eat at the fast food place there. My eyes had that gritty, swollen feeling from driving all night. I darked the windows and set my phone to wake me in three hours and, leaning my seat back, dissolved into sleep.

I slipped into a horrific nightmare in which I was bound by a huge snake that circled my arms and legs and wrapped its thick body around my neck. In front of me, another serpent was doing the same to Aurora. She reached out toward me helplessly. Her snake was so black it swallowed the pale light of the dream. I pulled with all my strength, straining to reach her, but the head of the black serpent appeared above Aurora's head, its red eyes blazing. It looked at me steadily, and somehow, I knew it was Thaumiel. He opened his ghastly mouth impossibly wide, venom dripping from his fangs and devoured Aurora's head whole.

Twenty-Three

I was to meet Aurora and Miranda at a B&B in Tacoma, Maryland, but they weren't there when I arrived. I settled into my room. Being a travel nurse, I had a routine when getting to a new assignment, but it seemed silly to go through all that when I would only be in this room for a few hours over a couple of days.

I hadn't even brought any scrubs. Scrubs are incredibly useful garments. You can wear the pants casually, and the sets are great for hanging around. Over the last few years, new companies had arisen in the scrub industry, mostly, I think, because people who were stuck at home because of the pandemic were wearing them all the time. They were a tiny bit more acceptable than sweatpants.

Aurora, who was three hours early, pushed her way into my room without knocking. She had an armful of paper grocery bags. Miranda, trailing behind her, had two six-packs of beer and a bottle of wine.

"Hope you're hungry," Aurora said without preamble. "There's a Senegalese place in Georgetown. I got tieboudienne and poulet yassa."

"With beer? I didn't think Senegalese cuisine would go with alcohol."

"They're not all Muslim, Paul, jeesh," Miranda quipped, giving me the stink eye.

I raised my hands in surrender.

"*Salaam alekhoum*," I intoned.

"Whatever," Aurora answered. "Any trouble on the road?"

"It was an uneventful ride except for the dreams."

"You stopped on the way?"

"Slept in the car."

"Were they visions, or . . .?" Miranda said, trailing off.

"He doesn't get those," Aurora replied. "Thomas gets visions. He has the sight, sometimes."

"So does James," I added.

We chewed in silence, each lost in their own thoughts. Miranda opened a beer and offered me one, but I shook my head.

"Everything all set for tomorrow?" I asked.

"There's chatter about the VP," Miranda said. "We don't think he's Returned?"

"He's a home-grown dickhead," I said. "A true believer. We think Thaumiel wanted him so he could use him as a vessel if something happened to the president."

"Wait," Aurora interrupted. "If we kill the president, he just possesses the vice president and takes office again."

"That's why we never thought about assassination, and why we forbade the Left Hand from doing it."

"There were plenty of people who were really pissed about that," said Miranda. "We had three teams ready, and they were told to stand down."

"Now you know why. What about the VP, anyway? Al Windig isn't turning over. He'd take a bullet for Roosevelt."

"The rumor is that he did, kind of, take a bullet. He doesn't wear any protective gear, because 'the pandemic is a hoax,' and we think he got bitten," Miranda explained. "No confirmation, just Marine One shuttling between the Naval

Observatory and Walter Reed."

I was flummoxed for a moment before remembering that the Naval Observatory contained the Vice President's residence.

"Could be a member of his family. He's got kids," I thought out loud.

"Could be," Miranda agreed. "I'm going to find out in a few minutes." She licked the peppery oil from the tieboudienne off her hand, then wiped it on a towel.

Aurora was straining, holding it together, but just barely. Miranda kissed her quickly, nodded at me, and was out the door before either Aurora or I could say something annoying like, "be careful."

We watched a pretty good karate movie without speaking and finished all of the food. Aurora looked at her watch obsessively. I tried and failed to distract her with some war stories from the seventeen hundreds.

"How are you holding up?" I asked finally, turning to my daughter and trying to keep my face neutral.

Her eyes filled, but she took a deep breath, made her face stern, and did not allow a single tear to fall. She only spoke when she was sure her voice wouldn't break.

"We would never be able to do this without the Left

Hand of God," she said at last. "She's so brave and smart." Aurora paused for a moment. "And utterly ruthless when she has to be."

"That's a little scary."

"It's wicked hot, is what it is."

I sighed like a long-suffering father, and she grinned.

"If Windig dies, though, that's going to screw up the whole timetable. They won't be able to have their trial on Monday," I said.

Aurora considered this.

She said, "They can't acknowledge it if he does die. They'd have to admit that the pandemic is real."

"They could invent some other cause of death, something heroic."

"They'd have to have a big state funeral and flags at half-staff, all that stuff," Aurora said and began pacing. "If Windig is dead, we've got a much better distraction than an explosion. One of us could be seen in public, looking like Windig. Roosevelt, or one of the other Returned would have to go right at him; they would know it was one of us."

"I could do it," I said, tapping a fingernail against my front teeth. "Hold a press conference or something public, something reasonably close to the south lawn, so that I could still wake the others if they need me."

"Like where?"

"The Holocaust Museum. Their 'scholars' have been trying to shut it down, saying it never happened, that it was a sham to get the world to accept the Jewish state."

She looked at me with utter incredulity.

"You're shocked? These people, these *monsters,* have no shame at all, Aurora."

"I keep thinking they have a bottom, a place they won't go below."

I chuckled bitterly. Over Aurora's shoulder, the muted TV showed protesters throwing Molotov cocktails at police in Chicago.

"As Peter is so fond of reminding us," I lectured, "we've seen this same rhetoric so many times before, the same rewriting of history, denial of what's clear from the record. 'Don't believe your eyes,' they tell their followers. 'It's all a manipulation of the communists or the deep state or the cabal of billionaires.' Napoleon did it. Hitler did it. Kings and popes throughout history have done it."

"When you describe it like that, it sounds an awful lot like religion."

"I'm aware of that," I answered. "Why do you think

we're atheists?"

"Peter isn't."

"Peter is Peter."

I was genuinely irritated, and I wasn't sure why. Augustine did not like changing plans at the last minute, but if the VP was dead —big if— Aurora's idea made sense. There was a wonderful irony in using their bigotry and fanaticism against them.

Aurora cocked her head.

"Miranda's back."

Twenty-Four

Miranda stumbled into the room, closed the door behind her, and leaned against it, catching her breath. The right side of her face was pink, with a black-and-blue mouse appearing over her eye. Aurora leapt to her, but Miranda pushed her hand aside. She looked furious and panicked and wild.

"Someone is going to be dead for this," Aurora said, taking Miranda by the shoulders and inspecting her face.

Miranda cupped Aurora's head and gave her a long, deep kiss. It was so raw and intimate, I had to look away.

When I turned back, their foreheads were touching, and Miranda was smiling a weary smile.

"No need to hulk out. I snapped his knee. He won't be causing anyone any trouble for the near future," Miranda said. She grabbed a towel from the bathroom and ice from the ice bucket and, applying it to her face, she began.

"We tried to get to Ward 71, that's the president's exclusive suite at Walter Reed. The cell leader assumed that would be where they would have taken the Veep. We all had scrubs and badges."

"That's where my white scrubs went," Aurora interrupted, and Miranda blew her a kiss.

"The badges looked great, but they didn't have a chip, so they weren't much help getting us anywhere. The elevators and corridors around Ward 71 were like an armed camp. Much more than usual, according to the cell leader. We weren't going to get close, so we hung out in the cafeteria and any break rooms we could access and listened for gossip."

"Kind of a long-shot with HIPAA," I said, and Aurora snorted. The vast majority of nurses I had worked with were slavish in their adherence to the national privacy law; you could get fired if you weren't. But sometimes there were loose lips.

Miranda touched her nose with her index fingertip.

"Everybody looked nervous or was trying hard for a poker face. The government's got that place locked down tight. The tidbit we did get was from one of the unit clerks. He was on a cigarette break and was whispering to someone on his cell phone in the alley. I bummed a cigarette from him and listened in. It's not a hundred percent, okay, but I'd bet all the money I could steal that the Veep is in there. Whether he's alive or not, I can't say."

We looked at each other, all calculating, analyzing the new information. Aurora was the first to look up from her reverie.

"So how'd you get the shiner?" Aurora asked at last.

"We ran into some cops on the way back."

"You snapped a cop's knee?" I asked.

"He asked to see my 'papers.' Can you believe that? In America? When I refused, he had me put my hands on the roof of a car parked beside the sidewalk, kicked my feet apart," Miranda explained.

Aurora said nothing, but she couldn't sit still.

"Then, you know, the usual," Miranda said, her face compressing to a line. "When he tried to feel me up, I told him to fuck off. That's when he hit me. He was alone, so I kicked back straight at his kneecap. I think I got the quad tendon and the patellar tendon. Anyway, the knee is toast."

Aurora nodded appreciatively.

"Look at you, throwing around anatomy terms," she said.

"Is it . . ., you know?"

"Hot? Oh, hells yeah."

"Good Lord," I said out loud. "You have your own room, for heaven's sake."

Miranda made a growling-purring sound, and the dirtiest smile I have ever seen on my daughter's face blossomed across it.

"Settle down for a moment," I said. "I don't have any way to contact Augustine directly. There's at least one cut-out between us."

"So you're going to do it?" Aurora asked.

I nodded.

Miranda scowled. "I don't know how many cut-outs. That's the point; none of us knows the full path from you to the others."

"So I'm calling an audible," I said. "That means you'll be on your own to get them to the OAS garage, at least in the first few moments."

"She won't be alone," Miranda said. "The Left Hand will

be everywhere."

"So will the Returned and their minions and all their sympathizers. The National Park police have okayed open carry in the District now," I said.

"In America," Aurora murmured.

"It's going to become a shooting gallery," I warned.

"We've got some vests," Miranda explained, "but no plate. And we have a metric fuck-ton of arms and ammo."

"This is not reassuring," I complained.

"Aurora made a spray for us all to keep off the bugs, but I could see hair at her temples turning gray when she did it."

"I can't give them enchanted vests," Aurora said miserably.

It was after midnight by the time I shooed them out. We had to be in Lafayette Park during the press conference the next day in case the infiltration went pear-shaped. Rioters, or so the caption labeled them, were being lined up against a concrete wall in Cheyenne.

I was too restless to sleep, though, so I stood in front of the full-length mirror practicing my Al Windig glamor. I found recordings of his speeches on the internet and practiced those as well. By three, I was done and ready to slip off when there was a soft knocking on the wall next to mine. I listened, embarrassed. Miranda and Aurora's room was behind that wall, and I was afraid I might be hearing unseemly sounds, but when the knocking came again, I knocked back.

I leaned my head against the wall, and I swear I could feel Aurora doing the same on the other side. Probably just my imagination.

"I love you," I said to the wall. There was no more knocking, and I finally fell asleep.

Twenty-Five

I got a couple of pork buns from a food truck on Constitution and tried to look like a tourist. I was wearing a pea coat and knit cap and holding my phone up all over the place to look like I was taking pictures. There were open seats on the bench in front of the Light Keeper's House, in the shadow of the Washington Monument. The traffic was lively, but not unusually so. While the press corps was, no doubt, frothing at the mouth for a chance to speak to the president for the first time in weeks, the rest of the city went on about its business.

Except for the special cops.

Roosevelt had created a special branch of Homeland Security called District Patrol. They had hats like the Chicago police, high-brimmed, with checkers above the bill. Their uniforms were navy and black. The pants were jodhpurs tucked into knee-high leather boots, and these folks were known for their brutality.

They reminded me of the Spanish civil guard: thugs in *tricornio* hats.

The media trotted out plenty of interviews with people who applauded their work in getting "undesirables" off the streets and making Washington safe for tourists and for shopping. Despite the good reviews, pedestrians and drivers alike gave these folks a wide berth.

So I was nonplussed when one started checking identification documents for anyone standing around the Light Keeper's House. Sure, I had phony papers, but it was the principle of the thing.

When he came to me he looked down, amused. He smelled of cheap aftershave despite already having a shadowy beard along his cheeks and chin. He didn't even ask, just held out his hand toward me.

"These aren't the droids you're looking for," I said, raising my hand in my best Obiwan and putting a little magic into the gesture. He nodded and moved on to the next person.

Aurora texted me that she was in position. She was in a crowd that had gathered near the First Infantry Monument behind the Eisenhower Building. She said the crowd was mostly Roosevelt faithful. No one had on bug protection. I reported that on the corner I was watching, it was about half and half. As soon as I texted this, a slim, middle-aged man in what looked like an expensive suit bent in half in front of me, clawing at his throat. Other people without bug protection ran to him. It was about thirty seconds before one of them did the same.

Miranda had a perch closer to the south lawn so she could see the proceedings, if only at a distance. I sat down on the bench again, pulling a tablet from my backpack. As it booted up, I put a protective barrier around me in a fifty-yard radius to keep the bugs out. I was immune, but people falling around me was distracting, and I needed all my concentration.

I was able to pull up two different broadcasts of the press conference. The camera held on an empty podium for a long time, before panning to the "gallery" of reporters. It looked for all the world as if a bunch of harried men and women were either madly scribbling or talking into earpieces.

A voice from off screen said, "Ladies and gentlemen, the President of the United States," at which point all the reporters rose. If I watched the screen on the right, the president's pet news network, I could make out some tiny edges of the green screen. On the other network's broadcast, the illusion was seamless.

Aurora texted: *So strange. People in green suits standing in front of the lectern. No seats, no microphones.*

I texted: *Can you make out our people?*

Aurora texted: *Negative. It's a scrum, but why? None of them are asking questions. Crowd here loving this, catcalling the press. Three down from bugs so far.*

I texted: *Two here.*

Roosevelt appeared at the podium, his luxuriant salt-and-pepper hair swept back, chiseled features perfectly lit. The audio sounded exactly like reporters asking to be recognized. The audio was different on the two different broadcasts, so they must have been reusing different old press conferences.

Out of nowhere, the podium rocked back and forth. The president stepped back, alert and composed. I couldn't see what was causing the movement.

Aurora texted: *One of the reporters just rushed him. He's in a green suit, so I can't tell who it is.*

That explained why it was invisible to the viewing public. Roosevelt waved the Secret Service away and held out his right arm. The flaming sword appeared in his hand.

"I know you're all interested in this," he said, brandishing it in front of him. "I'm as surprised about it as you are. You see, this sword was given to me by an angel of the Lord. The angel said it is a sword of righteousness, and so I will use it in righteousness." The flame went out, just as he swung at the air in front of him, and a red fountain appeared out of the air."

Aurora texted: *He cut the reporter's arm off. They're bleeding out next to the podium!!*

Roosevelt stepped back, wiping his shoe on the lawn. Two Secret Service agents dragged something away and another laid a throw rug down behind the podium.

"Our prayers have been answered, my friends, my fellow Christian Americans. God is on our side. Who have we to fear? I know it's a lot to take in, but the real Americans aren't even surprised. They always knew we were on the right path, God's path. All over the world, people are finally waking up to the truth.

"On Monday, the day we honor you hard-working Christian Americans, we are going to strike a great blow for God. We have already dealt the communist scourge of the Red Monks a blow, only yesterday, with righteousness." He raised his voice and lifted the sword over his head. "On Monday, we will see righteousness at work in the world once more. I don't want to spoil the surprise," he teased. "but we're going to take down one of the *big* bad guys."

Canned applause roared on both networks. Roosevelt hushed it, and the networks clumsily reduced the volume.

"I'll take one question from you vultures," he said. "You have already tried my patience and the patience of our country."

"Why did you kill her?" quailed a female voice from among the reporters.

Roosevelt looked at the spot from where the question had come like a man looking down the sights of a rifle. He held the intense gaze for a moment, then he smiled.

"You mean the communist libtard scum I brought to justice yesterday?" I guessed that the question wasn't about Barbara, it was about the reporter he had just killed on national television. Most of the folks at home, though, hadn't seen anything but a wobbling podium and a weird red spray.

"Her death was the beginning of the justice I will mete out against our dangerous, evil foe," he said and waved as he walked back toward the White House.

Aurora texted: *They're dragging away one of the reporters.*

I texted: *One of ours?*

Aurora texted: *No.*

I texted: *Then don't worry.*

Aurora texted: *What's happened to you?*

I shut the phone and lifted the shield. Two people immediately fell to the sidewalk, choking. I stepped around them to hail a cab.

Twenty-Six

That night, back at the hotel, I looked out at the city, the lights just coming on. Heavy, gray clouds threatened snow. Assuming my colleagues were now in the columns of the South Portico, I worried about what would happen to them if they emerged into snow. They would all be naked; you can't flow through rock with clothes on. We knew it would be cold, but no one had counted on snow.

If Thaumiel/Roosevelt had any power for the weather, I guessed that he wouldn't want it messing up his show. That he wanted to hold the trial and the execution outside was odd, really. There was so much more to control outside. I concluded that he must be drawing power from something beyond the White House. I just couldn't imagine what it could be.

People who don't know better say the waiting is the worst part, but the fear of what's to come is amenable to your will. You can master it with a lot of time and a lot of practice. Okay, most people, maybe.

Many people can master it.

I am lucky that I am able to master "anticipatory anxiety." That's what Andrew calls it. "Paying interest on a debt you don't owe." That's what Augustine calls it.

I wondered where Andrew had been reborn. I wondered how Augustine was keeping her mind occupied. Despite my mastery of anticipatory anxiety, I paced until I couldn't stand it anymore, then knocked on Aurora's door.

"It's open," came a voice from inside, and I wasn't sure which of them had spoken.

Miranda was cleaning a pistol on the desk, and Aurora was propped up in bed reading *High Times in Low Parliament* by Kelly Robson.

"Any good?" I asked.

"Oh yeah," Aurora replied. "It's a lesbian stoner buddy story."

"We *love* Robson," Miranda chimed in.

"That's nice," I said, crossing to the window.

"Room is on fire," Aurora murmured.

"I heard you. There's something not right outside."

Miranda killed the light in one smooth motion, then shoved the magazine into the pistol and chambered a round. Aurora moved to the window, lifting the corner of the curtain just enough to see out.

"Silver BMW, other side of the intersection," I said.

She nodded.

"One guy, looks like," she said.

"He's been there for hours."

"Maybe we should have a talk with him," Miranda added, slipping the gun in her pants at the small of her back.

Aurora touched her shoulder.

"If there's a guy who knows it's us, he won't be alone," Aurora said.

"Unless it's one of the Returned," I said. "But I doubt one of them would stake us out in a car."

Now it was Miranda's turn to peek out the window.

"I know that car," she said. "I've seen it before." She held out her hand without taking her eyes off the car, and Aurora gave her a collapsible monocular. "Government plates. I think it belongs to a congressman's chief of staff."

She closed the curtain slowly and texted on her phone. In a moment, she got a text back.

"I was wrong. The car belongs to someone from the White House communications office."

Aurora began throwing things in a bag. We were, once again, in a hurry. Our battle was less than forty-eight hours away; we couldn't afford to be taken now.

"You both know where to go?" I asked.

They nodded.

Aurora started to speak, but I cut her off.

"Don't tell me, and don't tell her," I said, indicating Miranda.

"Don't be such a fucking mansplainer," she shot back. "Of course I know not to tell her. I was about to tell you, before I was so rudely interrupted, that I love you. We'll get through this."

Yes, I felt like a total dickhead.

I wrapped her in my arms and took in a deep, quick breath through my nose. We stayed like that for a long time, only stopping when Miranda tapped Aurora's shoulder.

"I'll take some of that," Miranda said and smiled before flinging her arms around me.

When all the awkward clearing of throats and searching looks were done, I opened the door.

"Dad, are you going to be alright? You don't seem yourself."

"This is war, sweetheart. Sometimes I have to let go of the idea that I can save everybody. Some people don't want to be saved."

"Don't let the dipshits win," she said.

"See you on the other side," Miranda chimed in.

"I sure as hell hope not."

I checked into a Best Western in northwest DC, earning a smirk from the desk clerk because I didn't have luggage. I was using my VP glamor to see how it worked on real people, but the clerk didn't recognize me. I decided it was because he wasn't the observant sort. He had a baseball cap on that said MAKE AMERICA CHRISTIAN AGAIN on it, and, of course he didn't wear a bug net or gloves.

"Aren't you worried about getting sick?" I asked, picking up my room key card.

"It's a scam, brother," he said. "God gave me an immune system. You, too. Don't live in fear."

I passed through the lobby where an old man was

slumped over on the couch. He was wearing a tee shirt that said "Roosevelt Forever" and had a big gold cross on it. His blue tongue protruded from between his blue lips, his chest motionless.

"Clean up on aisle six," I called over my shoulder before stepping into the elevator.

Twenty-Seven

The sun rose at exactly the right angle to slip right between the curtains of my room's windows. My sleep had been fitful, unaided by the rhythmic thumping in the next room. I scanned the back parking lot through the slit in the curtains. No sign of the BMW. Now I was worried it had followed my daughter or her girlfriend. I flipped on the TV to see St. Louis and Oklahoma City in flames. The president had gone to DefCon 3.

I had two burner phones left and our protocol was clear; at this point in the mission only critical texts, and only use each phone once. I would have to endure the uncertainty a little longer.

The face staring back at me in the mirror looked awful. It looked old --not old-old, but middle-age old. The glamors and all the rest of the little magic I had been using was taking its toll. If I had to use a lightning bolt to wake someone up, I was going to come out of it with gray hair and a bigger bald spot.

Tamping down my anticipatory anxiety like an absolute champ, I went downstairs to avail myself of the continental breakfast, which consisted of stale Fruit Loops and muffins with so much preservative, that to eat one was to go back in time. I opted for the coffee, which was terrible, but hot.

A young couple talked excitedly at the far end of the room. They were in the standard issue preppy pastel polo shirts. He wore tan cargo shorts. She sported a baby blue tennis skirt. They were not wearing bug nets, despite the big sign that said "BUG REPELLENT, HEAD NETS, AND GLOVES REQUIRED." Live free and die, I thought, refilling the coffee. The good and strange thing about this pandemic was that it was not passed from person to person. You couldn't make anyone else sick if you wanted to go bareback amongst the insects.

That may have been why I was so cavalier about people

dropping around me. I had toiled for months saving or trying to save lives, and still there were folks who just walked around without any protection at all. *Vive la difference!* I rationalized my behavior by thinking that I was honoring everyone's right to be an idiot. In truth, though, I was simply bitter about all of it, and at that moment, in the "breakfast station" of the Best Western, I couldn't summon any hope at all.

I took the Metro from Columbia Heights to the Archive, changing cars after each stop to see if anyone followed. At Mt. Vernon Square station, I got off and waited for the next train. I finally emerged into the bright sunshine and bought a coffee at the chain coffee shop in the beautiful old brownstone.

From there, I made a loop using the open streets around the south lawn, changing my glamor with each lap. All was quiet on the White House grounds. I doubled back several times to see if I had someone tailing me, but there was no one that I could see.

On my last pass, I stopped at the William Tecumseh Sherman monument. It was about two hundred fifty meters from the south portico. I sat on the grass, the picture of an exhausted tourist, and reached into the ground, sending my senses through the earth. There were six warm sensations in the portico. The knights were all in place. When I opened my eyes, there were liver spots on the back of my hand. At first, I thought it was just the glamor, but it was on my real skin.

I was running out of magic, which was suboptimal. I made to return to my hotel room, but changed direction, moving across E Street and down 17th to the Organization of American States, where Aurora would be getting the garage ready for tomorrow's getaway.

This was a no-no, a bad breach of protocol. I was not to be anywhere near her until after the mission, but she was my daughter, and I'm stubborn. I decided I would check the area for the BMW, just in case, then head back to the hotel.

I walked down C Street, staring at a map I had pulled out of the garbage, and lingered in front of Constitution Hall, when I saw a Blue BMW illegally parked behind a dumpster across the street. I continued down C Street, then doubled back, coming up on the car from behind, using the hedge as a screen.

As I came around the end of the hedge, a hand grabbed me, and I was paralyzed. My vocal chords didn't work, and I couldn't move.

"Don't freak out," said a familiar voice behind me. I struggled uselessly against my bonds. "I want to talk, not fight, and I don't want to do it on the street. Will you get in my car if I let you go?"

My neck was suddenly able to move. I nodded. The vice holding all of my muscles let go. I shook out my shoulders and cracked my neck, drawing my magic up.

"Paul, we talk first, then we can brawl if you want."

I let go of the magic and punched him in the nose. His head rocked back, but he made no move to retaliate. He took a handkerchief from his pocket and sighed.

"Feel better now? Your daughter did exactly the same thing the first time we met, and she didn't even have a good reason."

"You were offering her up to Prentiss Gilchrist on a plate."

"Yes, well. That was then. Please, get in the car."

I walked around the back of the car, never taking my eyes off him, and slid into the passenger seat.

"What do you want, Jude?"

Twenty-Eight

"No small talk, then," Jude said, dabbing at his nose.

"After all the shit you've pulled, I'm finding it hard to believe you just want to talk."

Jude jerked his chin toward the OAS building.

"Someone tipped the District Patrol to your getaway. You need to change the pickup spot. Don't worry about Aurora. She saw the Patrol and slipped away."

"So why are you still here?"

"I was waiting for you," he said, looking me straight in the eyes. "I was pretty sure you'd check up on her. You followed her to the Ether, after all."

"Yeah, why's that?" I asked, and the magic swirled in my chest again. "Why are you tailing my daughter?"

"Paul," he said, his voice sharp. "I know how this looks, and I know what you think of me, but it's too important to waste time on these feelings. I've lived for years in the Ether. I know what their utopia looks like. I saw what they did with the Nazis, but by then I was in too far. They needed me, and I had to perform or they would let Lilith play with me."

Lilith had played with me, too, so I had nothing to say about that.

"After seeing what they did to Barbara, knowing what they're going to do to James, I can't stomach it anymore."

"What an inconvenient time to discover a conscience," I mocked. "Or is this just another con. If you go anywhere near Aurora again, I swear to fucking God, I will tear you in pieces."

"Paul, it's gone too far. Even I know that now. The only thing keeping the Returned from ruling this world is the insurrection back in the Ether. Some new species of sentient being is leading the cogs against the company. It's chaos."

"So why aren't you back there helping your masters?"

"You know what the Ether is like. You think I want that?"

"You did," I spat. "That's why we banished you."

Jude looked out the window, somewhere far away.

"Banishing me isn't going to help. You need to kill me," he said at last.

"Potato, potahto."

"The real death, the final death. You need to do that to me."

"If only," I replied, reaching for the door handle.

"Killing me will close some of the gateway, the door between us and the Ether, but it has to be permanent. I've found a way."

He had my immediate interest. If there was a way for him to die the real death, then maybe for all of us.

"What's the connection between your death and the gateway?"

"Our resurrection and the gateway are linked," he began. "I told you that Ibn Jumay opened the door when he resurrected us the first time. When we're all dead, it closes permanently."

"But the Returned are here."

"Some of them are here. They will all need to be sent back before we can close the door and put an end to this," Jude said. "They were banished to the Ether once; we'll have to do it again."

"You said they were too powerful. How are we supposed to send them back?"

"With guile," he answered and the smile on his face was the one I remembered, the one he wore before battle. His expression said he didn't care whether he lived or died.

"James's trial is in twenty-four hours, and I'm sure as hell not sharing our plan with you."

"Of course not," he said at once. "Can I help, though? Is there something I can do to show you I'm serious?"

So I told him. His eyebrows only went up once, but in the end he nodded.

"I've got to get busy," he said.

My door wasn't fully closed before he was racing out of the lot.

I unwrapped one of the burner phones.

I texted: *Change of plans, dear. I think we should donate blood before our big night out. Save a life and all that.*

One of the alternative escape sites was the blood donation center at the American Red Cross, but she would really have to hurry to get the vehicles there in time. If she got the text and agreed, she would respond, "I don't know, maybe."

I took the orange line to Foggy Bottom, but there were no texts on the phone when I got there. Perhaps she didn't get it or didn't have a chance to respond yet. Or maybe she had been taken, or worse.

It was dangerous to leave the phone on any longer, so I destroyed it there, miles from where I would be sleeping, dumping the two pieces in different trashcans before finally going to my hotel. The purchase of another burner phone was outside Augustine's operating instructions. We didn't have a safe vendor nearby.

That left me with one text on the remaining burner phone. I would have to keep that for last minute emergencies. Aurora was on her own. I wanted to scream or punch someone or jump up and down. I didn't do any of these.

I walked to a bar down the street and ordered a shot of Jameson, which I washed down with some beer that I had never heard of. It tasted like I was drinking lavender flowers and foam. As I was walking back to my hotel, I saw a man sleeping on a blanket on the sidewalk. He had a mangy dog curled up next to him. I threw him a bug protection spell that would last two or three days. As the magic left my body, my back tightened above my right hip. There was a shooting pain down my right ass cheek, and I groaned a little.

I was going to need a hot bath before bed. Not good at all.

Twenty-Nine

James pulled against the restraints. He was dreaming of slashing from side to side on horseback, the enemy falling away from him. She galloped through them, back and forth, like a needle through cloth, like the needlepoint she had done under the tutelage of her governess.

James was a woman when she first joined the order, and the others had covered for her because she was such a fearless warrior. Father Peter said he had never seen a knight as good with a flail. She called herself James, and ahorse, James preferred a sword.

He wheeled his mount, slapping his spurs into the

horse's side for another charge, and in the waking world, his feet tried to make the same motion, but the leather straps allowed him little movement. He swam toward wakefulness, only to be pushed under the water of sleep once more.

The only other person in the room was a bald man who sat hunching forward on a chair. The man's clothes were new, but they hung on him as if they had been made for a much larger person. His eyes were bloodshot, and his cheeks sagged.

Perpetua knelt before an altar to the Virgin Mary, a spray of devotional candles lit before it. Augustine knelt beside her, but Augustine was dressed in scrubs, not a habit.

"Sister?" Perpetua asked. "What are these clothes?"

She looked at the statue of the Virgin, and it was Augustine's face she saw. She stood, tripping backward. The crucifix behind the altar had been changed. The representation of Jesus had changed. Perpetua stumbled up the stairs of the altar, staring at the statue.

She knew that face. She had seen that face before.

"James," said Augustine's voice. "James."

Yes, she thought. That's his name. The face of the man on the cross is James. I know him. "This is blasphemy," she cried.

"James," Augustine's voice called as if she were searching for James, searching for her. Now she looked down from the cross above the altar, and he was James. He saw Perpetua, but he could not speak. His lips, his face, his body, were made of stone.

James's eyes opened to the dimmed room, to the bald man, who was drenched in sweat. The man stood up, wobbling. He pushed James back into the water, back into sleep.

Aurora emptied the last water bottle in one go and crouched among the trees at Freedom Plaza. It was way too hot for February. She had dodged District Patrol all night after seeing guards at the OAS building. It had taken all night to sneak into the garage and drive out the three vans which were now disguised as red and silver taxis and parked in front of Pershing Park.

When the time came, she would slip through Fraser House and extract the knights from the east. Her father would be on the other side of the White House, and she wasn't sure how she was going to get him after the raid, but she was confident he had a back-up plan. She only had one phone left, having used the other phone to check in on

Miranda. She followed protocol and destroyed the phone as soon as she knew Miranda was okay. The last phone had to be kept for an absolute emergency.

The vans were warded and safe for the moment. She couldn't see the south lawn from her position in the trees, but the roads in and out of the President's Park were jammed with trucks and people in uniforms.

Augustine pushed into the White House with her mind. She had taken care of patients with total paralysis before who could only move their eyes. She had thought it the most dreadful thing imaginable. Now she was living it, but she couldn't even move her eyes. She retreated to her mind and found she still had plenty of magic.

She had found James, called to him, called to Perpetua, his other self, but heard nothing in return. She could sense the others nearby but found the only mind she could touch was Peter. He was calm, but his thought betrayed a fatalism she had never felt from him before.

When she first approached him, he was chanting the rosary in his head. You can take the priest out of the pulpit, she thought.

"Augustine, is that you?"

"Finish your Hail Mary."

He finished the prayer.

"Are you ready to die?" he asked.

"I have died so many times, in so many ways. I am always ready to die."

"I don't have your experience."

"You've died a few times."

"Only four. You lot insisted I stay alive for the good of the council."

She could hear the wistfulness in his thought.

"Are you afraid?"

"I am not afraid to die and be reborn," Peter lamented, "but I am afraid I have wasted much of my time with you, all of you. I should have prepared better. I should have known this day would come."

"I blame myself, too. It's easy to get complacent after nine hundred years."

"Or just to get tired."

"Don't give up, Peter, and don't let the others know you feel this way. Be the rock."

"Augustine, I am afraid."

The feeling stayed there, trapped in stone.

"You're immortal. What do you have to be afraid of?"

"Not immortal, I think. To your question, I am afraid to fail, to fail all these souls, to fail our home."

"There is no failure. There is only the battle. We fight. We die. We fight again. We die again. There is only the battle."

Peter's thoughts went quiet. When Augustine heard them again, she heard, "As it was in the beginning, is now, and ever shall be, world without end."

Thirty

True to his word, Jude had arranged for a press release, security, microphones, and TV cameras for the Veep's big announcement of the closing of the Holocaust Museum so that it could be reopened as a museum of white history.

I thought he had overdone it, honestly. The idea was so cartoonish, so ridiculous that I was sure we had overplayed our hand. But at 6:00 p.m., when I arrived at the American Holocaust Memorial Museum, a crowd was already seated, the area cordoned off by Capital Police.

A lot of people were excited to see this sacrilege, and a wave of despair flooded me. I glimpsed the post-Returned world here on this plaza, and it was unspeakably ugly.

The podium was halfway between the two parts of Joel Shapiro's sculpture *Loss and Regeneration*. Seeing the circus we had arranged there was like watching someone take a dump on the altar of a cathedral. We were just running a con, playing at make-believe, but unless we succeeded today, I had no doubt some version of this atrocity was going to take place.

The limo had picked me up at the Eisenhower building, and no one was weird about it at all. I was sure that if the plan was going to fall apart, it would be at that moment. Someone would think, "Hmm I thought the vice president was at Walter Reed," and the jig would be up; we would be rumbled.

I missed James.

Independent thought, questioning of orders, these were things the current administration selected against in their recruiting, so all of the men in black were stoic doing their duty.

On the ride over, the radio said that protesters were returning fire on the army in Buffalo and that two bridges going into Jersey City had been demolished.

As I emerged from the car, people stood and applauded.

I waved the way I had seen Windig wave in the videos I had studied. It was the very picture of youthful enthusiasm, hand high over my head making sweeping semi-circles. It was big, big as a Nebraska sky. Someone in the president's pet news network had described it that way, and it had become the Veep's signature ever since.

The museum plaza wasn't very high up and looked directly into the trees on the south end of the National Mall, so I couldn't see anything of the "trial" on the south lawn. When the first of the knights emerged from their pillar, I would feel them. If I didn't feel all six, I was to bring a lightning bolt down right beside the portico, hopefully not killing James. The lightning was the Seneschal's Summoning and, like Pavlov's mutt, all Knights of the Order of St. John instinctively answered its call.

I got to the podium, cleared my throat, and realized I couldn't do it. I couldn't say what I had written down. I had eviscerated enemies, cut off limbs, set fire to barracks with men inside. But of all the despicable, detestable acts I had committed, none had repulsed me as much as a speech about replacing the Holocaust Museum with a paean to the history of the white man.

The crowd in front of me shuffled nervously. Far away,

a roar went up that reminded me of blood sports in the Old World. One man at the back turned to look over his shoulder for a minute, but no one else moved. They stared at me with an obscene fascination.

I took a sip of water.

"It's so nice to see all of you folks out here today," I said, vamping.

Protesters gathered in the mall across the street. The police held them back. One sign drew my attention like a magnet. It said HAVE YOU NO SENSE OF DECENCY?

That was the question that brought down the House Un-American Committee in the fifties. With a volley fired from across the table on national TV, Joseph Welch, a Boston lawyer, slayed the dragon that was Wisconsin Senator Joseph McCarthy with one sentence: "Have you no sense of decency?"

McCarthy became a pariah overnight.

This new McCarthyism, though, seemed to have no bottom. Rather than being appalled by a lack of decency, this new movement celebrated it, celebrated cruelty and recklessness, and some of its most fervent disciples sat in front of me.

"No one is saying it's okay to kill Jews. Let me get that

right out front before the press twists my words."

I squeezed the side of the lectern so hard that the edge began to crack.

"I've done my research. I have scoured the internet for the truth."

Lots of nods and crossed arms in front of me.

"Of course you can't believe a lot of what you read on the internet."

Scattered laughter here, more head nodding.

"I didn't pay any attention to those pinheads from fancy colleges who have nothing to do all day but eat avocado toast and find fault with our great nation. I listened to the *people*, to all of you. I used my common sense."

Here, the secret service dragged two people away who were in the last throes of anaphylactic shock. Another roar rose up behind the crowd, and this time several people turned, careful not to look at the bodies being loaded into a pickup truck.

"My research, my good, Christian sense, the mind God gave me, all say there is no credible evidence that the Holocaust ever happened."

The crowd was silent, and I felt tears falling from my cheeks onto the lectern. I also felt magical energy rolling toward me like a hurricane. Someone had taken notice of the ruse. Black cars skidded in front of the plaza, sirens screaming.

Then five blazing lights appeared in the distance. Five, not six. I raised my hand as if doing another big-as-a-Nebraska-sky wave. When I brought it down, a thick tree of lightning exploded on the south lawn, my glamor fell away, a sharp pain bored through my raised arm, and I collapsed.

Thirty-One

Like Barbara, James was brought out with a black hood over his face. He was supported on both sides by men in black, his legs rubbery beneath him. Roosevelt sat behind a high desk on the Truman balcony, towering over the whole proceeding.

Two floors below sat James. Next to him was a young woman nervously organizing papers on the table in front of her. Five meters to her right, another two men sat at another table. The jury sat on the first-floor portico, directly below Roosevelt. They were screened off by a series of translucent panels that obscured their faces. The press had the rest of the south lawn.

A heavy bell rang twice, everyone stood, and Roosevelt, resplendent in black robes, entered the balcony above. He smiled and nodded down at everyone, a kindly emperor smiling down on his subjects. Sitting down, he gaveled the trial into order.

A disembodied voice rolled over the crowd.

"What is my crime?"

All movement stopped. Roosevelt furrowed his handsome brow.

"What is my crime?" The voice was even louder, angrier.

"WHAT IS MY CRIME?!"

The ground shook with the sound. Roosevelt rose, his flaming sword appearing in his hand. Five pillars burned white in the evening twilight, and five figures floated free of the pillars. As the five lit on the ground, James began to glow, the hood dissolving to ash, the shackles on his hands and feet melting to slag.

In answer, seven beings of red flame appeared among the press, in the jury, and scattered across the grounds. Out of a clear, blue sky, a rope of lightning exploded on the lawn before the portico, spraying stone and earth in every direction.

A sixth pillar turned white, and a sixth figure floated free of the stone. He was carrying a huge, two-handed sword. His voice boomed again, shaking the earth.

"I am a knight of the Order of St. John of Jerusalem. Leave this place and never return."

The new figure punctuated his words with a whirlwind that swept up the Secret Service and soldiers surrounding the makeshift courtroom and flung them away to the south.

"Father Peter," Roosevelt said, his voice terrible as a wound. "You have come out of your hidey-hole at last."

Roosevelt leapt from the balcony, growing larger as he fell. He chopped his sword down toward Peter and the blades-that-were-not-blades met with a thunder so powerful two of the pillars cracked from the sound.

Over the heads of the press, Simon and Golachab were two blazing comets locked in aerial combat too fast for human eyes to follow. Thomas and Gamaliel were locked in a magical dance. Flames and water, wind and earth, flew between them until the ground opened beneath Thomas. As he fell, he rent the earth all the way to Gamaliel. The two sorcerers were swallowed up, and the ground sealed back together above them.

Reporters ran away from the portico but stopped at the

line of advancing troops.

James held two short, curved swords with which he struck like a windmill against Thagirion, who was too weak to do anything but parry the blows. One of James's swings severed the arm of Thagirion's vessel. The next blow cleaved his head from his neck. A black tornado appeared and Thagirion disappeared.

Augustine and Ghagiel fought with rapiers, blurring with movement. James ran toward her to attack Ghagiel from behind, when he was slapped in the chest by an invisible force, flying backward into a group of fleeing reporters.

A giant materialized in front of him. It was three meters tall with two heads, four arms, and four legs. A'arab Zaraq and Samael had fused the bodies of their vessels together. James rose, staggering, but Phil and Bart fell on the monster, arms and legs thrashing against the unholy thing in front of them.

Roosevelt-Thaumiel roared in a language that none of those present could name, and, as if pulled by a string, the knights flew toward each other. Thomas erupted from the ground. Simon fell from the sky. Thaumiel's flaming sword pushed against Peter's great sword, forcing him back with the others. Hundreds of men in black came streaming from inside the White House. The troops to the south continued their march, viciously beating the press and anyone else in their way.

"They all have magic," James said, catching his breath.

"Cogs," Thomas spat. "They've taken vessels."

"We will have justice at last!" cried Thaumiel.

A bullet of white light rocketed toward him. He blocked it at the last moment with his sword, and Aurora fell to the ground. She got to her hands and knees, then tried to rise, falling again before finally crawling to the other knights.

Thaumiel laughed, a sound filled with menace and madness.

"At last," he cried. "At long last."

The knights made a circle with James and Aurora in the middle.

"We fight to the end," Augustine growled.

"No," James said in a coarse whisper. "It's done. We can't beat them here, not today."

"We'll take as many as we can with us to the Ether, then," roared Simon, his body a living flame.

"No," James said again. "Let's take the bugs with us, end the pandemic. We can do that, at least. Let's not die for nothing."

"We are more than warriors," Peter said, his sword blinding against the encroaching gray. "We are healers. Today we have been bested as warriors, but not as healers."

Thomas sighed and began chanting. The others picked up the chant, although it did not get louder. James pulled Aurora to her feet, one of her arms over his shoulder. Although he could not hear her, her lips moved with the chant.

"Attack!" screamed Thaumiel.

"Attack!" echoed the Returned and their minions who rushed the circle of knights, who glowed steadily brighter. The energy of their circle incinerated the first attackers. Before any of them broke the circle, the blazing light that was the knights of St. John exploded upward.

The light shattered against the clouds, thin strands spraying in every direction. Everywhere, all over the world, tiny lights lit the air, as if a trillion fireflies had been simultaneously released. When the last sparks died, the mosquitoes that had killed so many millions were gone.

In the circle where the knights had stood, now there was fine, white ash, blowing away on the wind. The ground inside the circle was deeply scorched.

Clouds above parted to reveal a robin's-egg sky, and the

south lawn of the White House smelled like barbecue.

Thirty-Two

The moments after I collapsed at the Holocaust Museum are still blurry. As my vision was going dark, several shots must have hit the concrete beside me. I remember loud thwacks and stinging on my face. At some point, I was looking down the back of a charcoal gray suit coat, slung over the shoulder of the wearer.

The next thing was the sound of the road below me. I must have been in a car or a truck. When I woke up again, I was in a bed in a dark room. The shades were pulled tight. My arm was bandaged and seeping blood. My skin was saggy, and my chest felt heavy, like someone was sitting on it.

I slipped out of the covers and crept to the room's only door. Beyond it was a short stairway. The room swayed, and I clenched my stomach, preparing to vomit, before I realized that the room really was swaying.

I was in a boat.

The door at the top of the stairway opened into bright sunshine that blinded me. I crouched, hand over my brow to shut out the sun.

"Have some water," Jude said. "You lost a lot of blood. The shot might have nicked your radial artery. I sewed you up as best I could."

I followed the voice through the sun to a shady cockpit that was roofed with a thick, green tarp. Jude stood there behind the wheel. Little wavelets danced in the sparkling light. I grabbed a bottle of water from a basin filled with ice and drinks and drained it all at once, burping, before reaching for another bottle.

"Where?" I asked, falling to the cockpit bench.

"Lake Champlain," he replied. "We're headed for Canada."

"Border's closed and heavily patrolled."

"I know a guy."

My brain fog lifted slowly, and my thoughts went

immediately to Aurora and the others.

"Where are we meeting, and how are you going to keep them all from killing you?"

Jude clenched his jaw and said nothing, which made my heart jackhammer.

"Did we get James free?"

"No. Half the country is in flames. The New Orleans group had control of the river all the way to the gulf. They stole some helicopters and routed the guard. Then Roosevelt ordered tactical nukes. New Orleans is gone. The resistance folded after that."

I sat down hard.

"How many did we lose," I asked, my voice hoarse.

He clenched his jaw again.

"All of them. Aurora, too."

The air went out of the world, and I couldn't breathe. I only knew I had dropped the second water bottle by the cool splash on my foot when it hit the ground. My vision narrowed to a thin slit.

My brothers and sisters had been killed so many times, sometimes right in front of me. It was hard to see them go, but I knew it wasn't final, that we would meet again, even if it would be many years hence. The fact that I didn't know if

Aurora could be reborn was one part of what I felt. The other was that I could not bear, could not tolerate even the idea that she had been killed.

The water immediately around the boat began to boil before I felt Jude's hand on my shoulder.

"Easy," he said. "They took Ghagiel, Gamaliel, and Thagirion with them. There were too many possessed guards. They got rid of the plague in the end, just like Gallipoli. Peter is gone, too, I'm afraid."

I retreated to a place deep inside where it was cool and dark as the grave, where no sound, no thought, no memories could reach me. In this place, there were no doors or windows. I don't know whether my eyes were open or closed or if Jude said anything. I just went away.

The moon was rising when I was next aware. I still sat on the cockpit bench. Jude had rolled back the roof, and the boat was still except for the rocking of small waves. Scattered lights, like errant stars, surrounded us on the shores of the lake in every direction. Streetlights and sometimes a single lamp in a house window twinkled in the distance in every direction.

Jude came into the cockpit carrying two mugs of something warm. I accepted one. I hadn't realized my hands were ice cold until I held the cup.

"You did this. You helped them. You gave us up again," I said, but there was no fire in it. When you have lived and died and loved someone for centuries, it's harder to write them off.

"Yes," he replied and looked into his mug. "But we can end it, end it once and for all, once they're back."

"Aurora might not come back."

"Pretty sure she will be reborn or sent back the way she left."

"How could you possibly know that?"

"I met the guy she gave her Ether magic to. Very strange form, body, I mean, but he is incredibly powerful. He cares for her a lot. You, not so much."

"I killed the love of his life."

"So I hear. Those Returned that got sent back, they're stuck in the Ether, for a while at least. Faare and his people are fighting a pitched battle to hold them there. I think he wants to exact revenge on every branch of the Tree of Death. It won't close the gate, though, and they can't hold the Returned forever."

I splayed my hands and shrugged.

"Even Thomas never solved the puzzle of how to close

the door," I reminded him.

"He's going to be so pissed when he finds out that I have."

We were moving under the slow, steady power of the boat's inboard motor. When the engine stopped, we eased into a slip at the US side of the border crossing to find it well-lit and empty.

"I guess you do know a guy," I said aloud into the empty darkness. "I guess no one's going to start shooting, so let's get to Canada."

Jude froze, then lowered himself to the bench before reaching underneath it to retrieve a short-barreled shotgun. I followed his gaze to a figure in black tactical gear, full riot helmet with the visor down, M4 bouncing loosely on a shoulder sling. The figure approached, hands raised as Jude swung the shotgun to his shoulder.

The black figure stopped walking and pushed the rifle behind so that nothing was touching the rifle. Jude chambered a round, and then the shotgun became sand in his arms. His arms stayed out in front of him, but the gun was gone. Then he rose off the deck, hands clutching at his throat, feet kicking.

I leapt from the boat and sprinted toward the black

figure, but before I got within three meters, the face shield went up, and I stopped dead in my tracks.

"You okay, Dad? And what are you doing with this piece of shit?"

Dear Readers,

Thanks for spending some time with me and the Council of the Order of St. John. As you can probably guess, this isn't the end of the adventure for the K-Nurses.

I truly appreciate you taking the time to read my work, even if it wasn't for you. In that vein, I'd like to ask a favor. Whatever you thought of the book, good or bad, I will be in your debt if you could leave a review on Amazon.com or Goodreads.com.

Every review helps to establish the book's place in the literary world and makes it possible to keep the series going.

I hope it gives the general public some insight into the tremendous challenges nurses face today. Everyone says nurses are heroes, but that sentiment has become hollow and a poor excuse for the kind of support nurses really need. They give of themselves even when they are discouraged and burned out. If this book gives you a little peek into their world, so much the better.

Thanks for reading and all my best wishes,

Mark Leo Tapper

Other K-Nurse books available from Amazon.com:

The Road to Damascus: K-Nurse 1
The Left Hand of God: K-Nurse 1.5
But a Wandering Voice: K-Nurse 2
The Singer of Thrace :   K-Nurse 3
Between the Dragon and His Wrath: K-Nurse 4
In the Wilds and Mountains I Hunt: K-Nurse 5
In Thy Absence   K-Nurse 6

Mark Leo Tapper is the Award-Winning author of *The Vials of Our Wrath*. He lives, works as a nurse, and writes speculative fiction from the home he shares with his wife Susannah, stepsons Arthur and Felix, and several STET pets.

You can find out more about the author and his books at MarkLeoTapper.com. Sign up at the website to receive news of events, new K-Nurse releases, and download deals.

The audiobook of **The Road to Damascus**, narrated by Phil Thron, is available from Audible.com

Made in the USA
Middletown, DE
25 November 2022

15619408R00120